I sincerely hope that you enjoy reading Northern Knights.

Ed Pahnke

Northern Knights

by

Ed Pahnke

This book is a work of fiction. Places, events, and situations in this story are purely fictional. Any resemblance to actual persons, living or dead, is coincidental.

© 2004 by Ed Pahnke. All rights reserved.

No part of this book may be reproduced, stored in a retrieval system, or transmitted by any means, electronic, mechanical, photocopying, recording, or otherwise, without written permission from the author.

First published by AuthorHouse 08/02/04

ISBN: 1-4184-5563-6 (e-book)
ISBN: 1-4184-2865-5 (Paperback)

This book is printed on acid free paper.

To my wife, Rosemarie. Without her help, this novel would not have been possible.

CHAPTER ONE
EVERYONE CAME FOR THE WEDDING

Will Scathlock stood at the second floor window of the Church at the Corners, staring outside. "Five automobiles just now turned off the trunk highway, probably full of more folks comin' to your wedding."

Bob Brunet looked up, but he didn't answer. Nervous, he smooth his thick, brown hair before digging his hand into his trouser pocket and twisting the gold wedding ring between his fingers. Will Scathlock, his best man, refused to carry it, declaring, "I don't do good in front of folks. I'd surely lose it or drop it or something."

Bob loved Marian Alcott, but he couldn't stop thinking of reasons not to marry her that day. Weather couldn't be one of them.

That September tenth in 1932 was a perfect Saturday. No clouds marred the blue sky on that early afternoon, and soft, pine scented breezes wafted through open casement windows. They played about the steeple of the Church at the Corners. More properly called the First Congregational Church of Langston, the white clapboard building overlooked meadows and wood lots. The Moose Ear River lay to the east and the trunk highway to the south. To the north, a quarter of a mile away, the village of Langston dozed.

At the window, Bob said, "I count five more automobiles."

Will turned to him. "That's what I just said. You must've heard me, or why else would you've come over here?"

The line of automobiles labored along the dusty county road leading to the church. They followed each other so closely that they reminded Bob of a Fourth of July parade. With the tiny parking lot packed with flivvers and farm wagons, the new comers would have a tough time finding room to park, let alone get inside before the ceremony started.

A head taller than his squat, mustachioed best man, Bob stood next to Will while they talked. He was especially glad to have Will to talk with.

"Is something troublin' you, Bob?"

Bob stared at the pine floor. Not knowing where to begin, he simply voiced his doubts. "I love Marian." A wisp of a smile crossed his lips. "But this really doesn't seem like the right time to marry. People have been thrown off their land by that bastard, John King, and need help. He's probably eyeing my property. I hope I don't have to sell more land to come up with the dough to pay the next tax bill, let alone mortgage payments."

"You know you can count on my help," Will said

"Judging from the way John King took over running the bank, he's making the most of Richard's kidnapping to enrich himself. It's hard to believe John and Richard are brothers. The only thing they have in common is they both smoke pipes."

"They were at odds even before Richard took control of the bank," Will said. "What are you getting at?"

Bob continued to look at the floor. "If we could ransom Richard King from his kidnappers, he could run the bank the way he did before. That'd be swell, but a fifty thousand dollar ransom will take months to raise, and maybe his kidnappers won't wait that long. There's so much to do. What if I don't give Marian all the attention she deserves? With everything else going so wrong, how can our marrying be right?"

"Your dad was fightin' Quennel five years ago, before he died," Will said.

"And I've blamed Gil Quennel for Dad's death ever since. I know he didn't cause the train accident, but I can't help feeling Dad should never have been on the train."

"But, Bob, him and your dad was fightin' over that parcel of land for months."

"Yes, and Quennel got hold of the land and blocked good folks from their own fields. They lost everything."

"Did you hear what happened to the parcel of land by the Moose Ear that you sold to pay the taxes?" Will said, shaking his head sadly. "Quennel got hold of it, too. He's got land 'longside o' you now, but what can you do to stop him? He's got too much money. You think him and John King's workin' together?"

"It wouldn't surprise me. I promised Dad I'd fight Quennel and his gang, and I have. Gamwell County'd be better off without his scheming and conniving. This Depression and Quennel were bad enough, but now John King comes along."

"I can think of scores of reasons not to get married," Will said. "I always have. That's why I never got married, but I thought you had your mind set. You claimed you'd marry after you graduated from that college in Eau Claire, left me and Joe in charge of your business. I remember you saying that you and Marian'd have more in common if you went back and finished up." Will puffed out his chest. "I done all right with a third grade education. Life's learned me everything I need to know, but that's me. Now your schooling is behind you. As for today, maybe we should light out while Marian's walking down the aisle."

Bob raised his gaze from the floor to Will's face. Again Bob plunged his hand into his trouser pocket and touched the wedding band he planned to put on Marian's finger.

"You're nervous," Will said. "All o' them problems have been here for a while. Solve 'em and new ones 'll pop up. You and Marian are meant to get married today. Otherwise, you'd be out tramping over the countryside right now."

"I suppose," Bob said. "But..."

"No buts," Will said. He changed the subject. "I thought everyone was here already. I don't know why folks come so damned late."

"Somehow, I wish they'd never get here," Bob said.

In another room in the church, Marian Alcott stood while Alice Blue relaxed on the divan. Having whirled around before the mirror countless times, Marian thought it would be a welcome relief not to see her own reflection. She studied the mirror for a minute. It was connected to oak posts by pegs. She stooped, grabbed the bottom of the mirror, and flipped it over to face the wall. There was no response from Alice.

Marian sighed, brushing back her auburn hair, then twisting the blue-green aquamarine brooch pinned to her gown. Bob had told her he bought the brooch because the blue-green color of the aquamarine reminded him of her eyes.

"I love Bob," she said suddenly. "I enjoy looking into his deep blue eyes, but…" Marian hesitated. "Alice, do you think I was too hasty in accepting his proposal?"

"You must have doubts. Otherwise you wouldn't ask. The clock's about to strike twelve, so to speak. It's only natural to be uneasy." Alice stood and smoothed a wrinkle in her Nile green dress while she spoke. The dress came directly from the Sears Catalog for $9.98, a trifle more than Alice had wanted to pay, she had said. She lifted the silk taffeta hem and revealed a trim ankle and calf in French nude silk hose, her color. Judging from her expression, she admired the fit. Of course, the seam was straight. "You should consider yourself lucky. You don't have the family opposition Mike and I have to face. I hope that I have a big wedding and a gown like yours, someday."

Marian wore a wedding gown of clinging white satin with the train attached to bias-cut hip yoke. The gown suited her willowy figure, nearly two inches shy of Bob's six feet. "I'm sure everything will work out for the two of you, and Bob and I are lucky, but am I prepared to be Bob's helpmate after shepherding classes of children about? I'll miss teaching too." Marian had to give up her teaching position. Because of school district rules, married women were not allowed to teach. "No doubt I'll have responsibilities, but Bob's so intent working in the community that I'm afraid I won't measure up to his standards. I don't want to have his love before we're married and lose it afterward."

Marian swept past Alice to the open window. The breeze ruffled her hair. She gazed across a lot chock-full of black Model T's and farm wagons toward the trunk highway two miles away. Five automobiles all but halted at the crossroads before turning onto the rutted dirt road that led to the church.

"More guests," Alice said, looking from her vantage point.

"Somehow, I don't think so. I wish we were finished with the ceremony."

"Ha. I don't think you know what you want, Marian Alcott. A minute ago you weren't sure you wanted to get married. Say, who turned the mirror to the wall?"

The strains of the "Wedding March," a trifle tinny, played on an upright piano caught Bob's attention. He opened the door and motioned Will to go ahead.

Bob stepped out onto the landing. His glance wandered to the three hewn spruce beams that spanned the room. A huge chandelier crafted from white pine hung from each one. From the hubs of each, eight spokes radiated outward. They held bronze lanterns that had been converted to electricity when the power line from Langston had arrived.

In the hall below, the crowd of people sat facing away from him. Even from the back, Bob recognized each friend, neighbor, and relative.

Among the friends was Celeste King, wife of the kidnapped banker. Her red hair gave her away. She couldn't tuck it all under a cloche.

All the folks were freshly scrubbed, but many wore clothes that were frayed or patched. Bob didn't embrace a person because of wealth or social status. He himself was land poor, he had much land and little capital with which to improve it, but there wasn't much money in Northern Wisconsin's Gamwell County.

While they walked along the landing, Bob and Will straightened their red and blue polka dot ties and buttoned their double-breasted blue, worsted suit coats. The leather of their new black shoes creaked with each step. Doubtless, both men would have been more comfortable in dungarees and brogans.

Bob rubbed his hand along the railing before descending the wooden steps, and he thought back to his youth. It had been fifteen years since old Reverend Duncan had expelled him and a group of boys for sword fighting in the loft. In their imagination, it was a castle turret.

"We'd best hotfoot it down to the altar before Marian gets there," Will said.

After climbing down the worn wooden steps, Bob and Will took their positions opposite Reverend Mike Rood. To say the Reverend was a big man was like calling a boulder a pebble. He had graduated from the rough and tumble life of the lumberjacks five years before. Usually docile as a Saint Bernard, he could be riled, and then, look out.

"Relax, Bob," Reverend Rood said. Beneath his thinning, pale yellow hair, his broad forehead shone in the sunlit church.

Ed Pahnke

Bob and Will stood facing Reverend Mike. Bob's hands felt moist, his mouth dry. A glass of beer would have tasted mighty good right then. The tone of the music changed. Bob glanced over his shoulder and saw Marian followed by Alice walking down the steps from the loft. Taking a deep breath, he resigned himself to married life.

CHAPTER TWO
UNWELCOME GUESTS

Bob fidgeted while Marian descended from the loft, her gown brushing both the balustrade and plaster wall. Saucy smile, bouncing blond hair, and all, Alice Blue followed her. Marian's sober expression changed when she reached the main floor. A forced smile showed on her full lips. Her white pumps tapped a dozen times while she walked on the white pine planks of the floor. She stopped, and Bob froze. Were there doubts in her mind too? Why else did she hesitate?

When Alice caught up with Marian, Bob knew why she had stopped. Alice picked up the train of Marian's gown. After walking another dozen steps, Jeffery Alcott, Marian's father, took her arm. She clutched a bouquet of white roses in the other. They began their march down the center aisle. Stuffy old Alcott appeared somehow like a marionette as he thumped alongside his daughter. Whispers of approval met Marian when she passed each row of wooden benches.

Ed Pahnke

To Bob, hoping time would stand still, the "Wedding March" resembled a dash down the aisle. In a moment, presto, only a step separated Marian from him. He reached out his hand. Jeffery Alcott gave him Marian's hand. The sweet perfume of Marian's roses, or perhaps a scent she wore, excited his senses.

Reverend Mike Rood winked at Alice. She blushed and walked to her side of the altar. Bob and Marian turned and stood directly in front of Reverend Rood. The expression on his bride's face appeared as though it had been chiseled there during an inquisition, and Bob suspected he looked much the same. Moist hands entwined, they stared straight ahead into space beyond Reverend Mike Rood.

Reverend Rood smiled while he prepared to begin the ceremony, and his smile was infectious. Bob and Marian broke into uninhibited grins. The music stopped. When it did, Bob felt that the people edged forward in their seats, the better to hear and see.

The two doors in the rear of the church slammed open against the walls, and everyone's head turned from the ceremony.

A squad of men led by Sheriff Roland Blue, Alice's father, strode down the aisle. Dressed in a white silk shirt, black vest, and black trousers, he presented the appearance of a tough professional. Gil Quennel limped stride for stride with the sheriff.

"Hold everything," Sheriff Blue shouted.

A barrel of a man, Roland Blue was nothing like his dainty daughter. His head sprouted from his shirt collar like a big toe. Except for a pug nose and a shock of brown hair, his face appeared to be painted on his head. But Roland Blue was not to be taken lightly.

Before Roland and Gil had walked half way down the aisle, Bob had dropped Marian's hand. His face red from embarrassment and anger, he stood facing them while they approached him.

"I'll handle this, Marian."

Alice rushed to Bob's side. "I am so sorry about this, I had no idea."

"Don't fret. I'll see what that son of.., your father wants."

"Hold your temper, Bob," Marian said. A frown creased her brow.

After taking several quick, deep breaths, Bob felt somewhat composed, and he started up the aisle to meet Blue and Quennel.

When he stopped, he said, "I'm sure both of you are strangers to a church, so let me instruct you how to act."

"Don't waste your wit on me, Brunet. I'm here on business. I'm placing you under arrest for theft."

"Theft! Except for Marian's heart, I haven't stolen anything." Bob fixed an unwavering stare on the sheriff.

His lips hardly moving, Blue replied, "Squire Quennel says different."

A chorus of hisses resounded from those assembled for the wedding at the name "Quennel." He'd been buying foreclosed properties for pennies an acre, and the sheriff then considered the former owners squatters if they were still on the property. Gil Quennel gave the sheriff orders, and the sheriff evicted the former owners.

"Quennel. I should have known you would be at the bottom of something like this." Bob's anger reddened his face, but he spoke calmly.

"Did you trump this charge up because I refuse to call you squire like you expect of everyone else?"

More usurper than squire, he had let it be known that he expected and was entitled to be called squire because of petty political appointments, wealth, and large land holdings. Bob felt that any time he spent knocking Quennel off his lofty perch was time well spent.

Bob continued, "I'll treat everyone to a round of drinks after the wedding, tea for you, Quennel."

Quennel stiffened for a moment but quickly regained his aplomb. A tall, wand like man, he had thinning brown hair and a hawk like nose. Ten years older than Bob, he and Bob had been adversaries for as long as anyone could remember. Dressed suitably for the position of "country squire", he wore a tan, plaid Norfolk Jacket, medium gray trousers, and saddle shoes.

He calmly adjusted his navy and brown striped four-in-hand with his right hand while leaning on his blackthorn cane. "After today, the only bars you'll see will be those on your cell door and window."

The smirk on his face quickly melted when Bob lunged at him, but Quennel lashed out at Bob with his blackthorn cane. Quennel had served bravely in the World War I and was wounded in the right leg. He missed Bob with the cane, and it smashed down on a wooden pew. In close, Bob connected on his chest with a roundhouse right, but the man did not waver. He grabbed at Bob but missed.

Quick and agile, Bob danced around him. Suddenly, when Bob was between steps, Quennel brought his cane down on Bob's foot. Pain shot up his leg, and he hobbled off to sit in a pew. While nursing his foot, Bob yelled out, "Join in, folks. Let's make this a wedding to remember."

Northern Knights

The invitation wasn't wasted. Wedding guests became a mob surrounding Quennel, Blue, and his deputies. The sound of gnarled knuckles smacking against flesh replaced the "Wedding March." Two men rushed Blue, but he caught them by their wrists and banged them together like symbols. When they collapsed, he looked around the room for Bob.

After inviting the crowd to join the fray, Bob slid along the wooden seat to the outside aisle. Will Scathlock had been standing dumbfounded next to Marian since the melee began. They had stepped up on the chancel to watch the commotion.

Bob stood on the wooden seat and motioned to Will, but Marian saw him first and poked Will. Amid the shouts, fights, and screams of women, Will sidled along the wall, unnoticed, to where Bob waited.

"Up to the loft," Bob said.

"But, Bob."

"No buts, as you once remarked. Out of jail, I know I can prove I'm innocent. Inside, I won't stand a chance. The Manitou Hills won't question us. There's forest and stream enough to hide us, and game enough to fill our bellies.

"Are you with me?"

Will shook Bob's hand. "Hurry," Bob said. "Up to the loft."

The two comrades dashed unseen up the steps to the loft. There was a closet beyond the rooms where they had waited for the wedding to begin, and Bob knew from his boyhood escapades that a seldom-used trap door in the ceiling opened to the belfry. Bob stifled a sneeze when they entered the closet. Aside from dust and cobwebs, it was empty.

After closing the closet door, Bob gave Will a boost. He pushed the door open and climbed up and onto the belfry floor.

When he looked down, Bob motioned him to close the trap door. "I want to stay here and listen," he whispered. He thumped on the wall. "Did you hear that?"

Will nodded his head.

"When I thump again, you open the door and pick me up, quick."

As the trap door shut, Bob opened the closet door a crack to listen. Then he crept out to watch.

When Bob had stood on the pew to motion to Will, Reverend Mike Rood had been standing behind Will and Marian with a bewildered look on his face, but he was no longer bewildered. He exploded.

"There will be no more fighting in the house of God," he yelled.

Rushing into the fray, he separated combatants by simply walking between them and pushing them down like stalks of corn. Not until he reached Sheriff Blue did he halt. "Will you stop this brawl?" he said.

In response, Sheriff Blue yanked his revolver from his holster, pointed it heavenward, and fired. Reverend Rood would have a devil of a time collecting money from the county to fix the roof. Bob smiled grimly.

The explosion still echoed, but the fight had ceased, more quickly than by any orders or threats.

"Where's Bob Brunet?" Roland Blue bellowed.

Reverend Mike gave Blue a sharp look for his behavior.

"He's gone out the back door," someone said from the crowd.

As though the word of God had been heard, the anonymous someone was believed. The sheriff gathered his men and trooped outside.

No worse for the skirmish, Quennel smiled while brushing off his jacket and slacks with one hand. With the other, he tapped his blackthorn cane on the pine floor.

Whistling "Mademoiselle from Armentiers" he strolled outside. Perhaps he was thinking that, captured or not, Bob Brunet would no longer be troublesome to him. He took a deep breath and seemed to relish it.

Bob turned and hurried to the closet. He promised himself he'd wipe the haughty expression off Quennel's face one-day soon.

CHAPTER THREE
HE JUST HAD TO SAY GOOD-BY

Bob kicked the closet wall.

Will lifted the trap door and reached his hand down to Bob. Bob concentrated when he jumped to grab Will's hand; he tried several times before catching hold of Will's hand. A yank got him to the two by eights forming a framework around the trap door. When one hand was firmly clenched on the floorboard, Will let go of the other hand. A grimace and two grunts later, Bob sat on the dusty belfry floor. Both men kept low to remain out of sight.

"I been fightin' birds and bats, two of 'em, since I got up here. You'd think bell ringing would scare 'em off; but they got shelter, the birds that is." While speaking, Will lowered the trap door silently into place. "I'm glad of one thing, no wasps."

His voice low, Bob said, "I never got up here when I was a kid, too short. Finally made it." He looked about him at the peaked ceiling, rafters, and wall studs. "I heard folks shuffling out of the church. Blue and his bozos left long ago, but I don't know about Quennel.

"We'll have to wait a while before the church parking lot clears out. Take a peek over the window sill to see what's going on."

Will slowly edged his head above the weathered, wooden sill. His gray eyes and pointed nose were in full view, if somebody had cared to look. "Some people are starting cars, and some folks is busy running around keeping out of the way of moving automobiles and wagons. Sardines got more room than folks in those flivvers and wagons. The Grinells are on their way toward Langston in their two Chevrolet sedans, but Joe's starting your Nash touring car. Some of those black Ford Model T's must date back to 1915, and most of 'em's stuffed with people.

"We got a while before the crowd's gone, Bob." Will eased himself down behind the wall. "Do you suppose Joe cares that we ain't with him?" He spoke softly in a monotone. "Even though he's your foreman, I never got real close to him."

"I knew Joe Worman in high school. Why, we played baseball together. He may be a little too ambitious, always wanting more money, but he's a dependable worker.

"I don't know about him. Sometimes I think he don't like neither of us too much. For that matter, why didn't we take your car?" Will asked.

"I thought about a quick escape, but I figured Blue would put out a call describing my automobile. I'm sure he'll get the license number, too. We'd have to abandon the car near the hills, and that would give our general location away. If we left on foot instead of climbing up here, we would've been caught and tried by now. After we leave, we'll be free to hike without being caught.

"For now, we can take time to relax. When we get down, I've got to contact Marian, tell her not to worry."

"She ain't the only one worrying," Will said. "I don't know what I was thinking about when I agreed to get mixed up in this fugitive business. Do you honestly think you can clear yourself with the kind of hand Blue, Quennel, and King hold?"

Bob thought for a moment. "There are cards and there are card houses. Remove one card from a card house and the house crashes down. When we find that card, we'll topple Quennel, King, and Blue.

"The mystery is, where do we find Richard King? When the card house tumbles, we need him to build it back up again."

"I hope those fellows don't have their card house stuck together with cement. They won't be so easy to topple then," Will said.

Both men sat on the floor leaning against a wall. Bob closed his eyes and thought about Marian. Happy that she was safe, he knew he'd never wish the life of a fugitive on her. Digging his hand into his trouser pocket, he twisted the gold wedding band that was to have been Marian's between his fingers. In his imagination, he felt her touch, saw her smile. His own smile faded. It seemed like a week since he had last seen her. Would it be a lifetime before he saw her again?

At least Bob's mother didn't see him become a fugitive at his own wedding. She would have been holding back tears. Later, he'd be able to calmly explain that he was no criminal. He could ease the shock. Bob's mind wandered to his rugged father. He had died in a railway accident while

Northern Knights

Bob was at college. When he died, Bob had quit school to take over the family business, but he had gone back later when things had settled down.

He looked across the belfry at Will, remembering:

Seven years earlier, he and Will had become fast friends during the final log drive on the Moose Ear River in Northern Wisconsin. Young and inexperienced, they yearned for adventure. Driving logs was one of the most dangerous jobs around, but the young men craved the experience of being "river pigs." Though not up front in the drive, their job in the rear, nevertheless, was dangerous, as the number of men killed and maimed over the years testified. Bob and Will had to sack the rear, push logs that had floated into still water out into the current. Bob was maneuvering a log with a peavey when the log bucked back. The peavey hit him on his nose, breaking it and throwing him, dazed, into the water. Will jumped in after him. A few tugs got Bob to shore, and a little first aid had gotten him back into the drive.

From that time right up until that instant, their friendship had grown.

An hour passed before Will peeked over the sill. "The lot's empty. There ain't no automobiles on the county roads that cross in front neither. If we got to go, I suppose now's as good a time as any to leave."

"I like your consistent attitude," Bob said, "always a crape hanger, never jolly."

"It's my nature, but maybe we can win out." Will's expression contradicted his words.

"Sure we can. Those louses won't get us down, but we have to get ourselves down, from this belfry, I mean. There's a telephone in Mike's office. On second thought, I'll write to Marian. It'll be easier for both of us. Besides, I don't want to talk to Jeff Alcott now of all times." Bob stood up.

"Please call Joe, and tell him we'll be by soon to pick up some clothes, boots, and guns. I'll be scoutin' around outside. As soon as you finish, we're off."

After jumping down from the belfry, the men crept down the steps from the loft. They might as well have thumped down the steps. Nobody was in the church. Will hurried through the nave past the chancel to Reverend Mike's office.

Relaxed, at last, Bob stretched his arms while walking out of the church, alone instead of with Marian. Outside it was quiet. The sun had begun its afternoon descent. After going down the wooden steps, Bob stood mulling over his next move. He kicked at the dirt, and a film of dust settled on his black shoes.

"You rushed off so quickly before that I didn't get a chance to say good-by," a nasal, grating voice said from behind Bob. "It's a shame that you won't be able to kick up your heels at your wedding like you thought you would, Brunet."

Bob recognized Quennel's voice and swung about to face him. He glowered, but Gil's thin lips were curled into a mocking smile. "Quennel, you here? How did you know w…?" Bob stopped before he said "we." "where I'd be?"

"I didn't, but I took a chance. If I'm wrong, Sheriff Blue is hounding you, but if I'm correct… As you see, I am. I know you so well it's scary sometimes. We've been enemies too long. It's time to end the feud. Today, I'll be rid of you."

Bob backed away from the church. Quennel pressed forward, his limp barely perceptible. In one hand he clutched his blackthorn cane, in the other, a Colt revolver.

"You stole from me," Gil said.

"That's not true."

Paying no attention to Bob's answer, he continued stalking Bob. "I'm not going to shoot. That would be murder, but don't test me. I want you in jail."

I'm not ready to go to jail, Quennel. As a matter of fact, it's likely you'll be locked up long before me."

Bob tried not to look at Quennel. He didn't want to tip him off that Will was closing in behind him. While Will descended from the wooden stoop, Bob prayed there would be no telltale creaks. Good ol' dour Will. Nobody could take his place. Bob's heart thumped as though he had been running a race while, step by step, Will stole up behind Quennel. Two more steps. He faltered, almost stumbled, and stopped. No time to tumble now, but Will regained his balance.

Quennel kept his attention on Bob, but for how long. With only three feet between them, Will rushed headlong at Quennel and smashed into him with all of his two hundred plus pounds. At the same time, he wrenched the Colt from his hand. The revolver skittered across the rutted dirt. Off balance, but still on his feet, Quennel lashed out with his cane, and laid it across Will's left shoulder. Quennel raised his blackthorn cane again, but Bob thundered toward him and left hooked him to his jaw. Quennel dropped his cane and staggered back. Arms flailing, Bob crowded him with upper cuts. Gil tried left jabs to no avail. While Bob kept Quennel off balance, Will retrieved the Colt.

"Hold it," Will said.

Bob stepped back. Quennel scowled at Will.

"I'll tie him up, Will."

"We got no rope."

"We'll lock him in the cloakroom in the church."

"Bob, the church ain't got no locks."

"I'll figure out something. March, Quennel," Bob said.

For his part, Quennel brushed back his hair and adjusted his tie. Before moving, he said, "You've not seen the last of me. I intend to see you jailed."

"Move," Bob said and picked up the blackthorn cane. "Quennel, I don't like seeing you so glum." He grinned. "I think a stay in the church cloakroom will go a long way toward giving you a more sunny disposition."

Bob and Will hustled Quennel into the church. He objected when Bob motioned him into the cloakroom until Will pulled back the hammer of the Colt. Quennel shuffled inside. Will swung the heavy oak door shut, and Bob propped a chair against it.

Loudly, Bob said, "Your cane will be outside the door. For your own protection, I'll keep the Colt for a while."

"I'll get even with you," Quennel's voice sounded muffled.

"He won't break through that door. We'll have plenty of time for a clean getaway," Bob said.

"Let's not waste time patting ourselves on our backs. Let's move on. I wonder where Quennel put his Auburn Speedster. I sure admire that automobile." The shadow of a rare smile flickered across Will's face.

"Could be anywhere. Ol' Quennel has the best. Did you ever know anyone else who lived in a chateau? As rich as he is, you'd think he'd try to do some good instead of wanting more."

"He ain't you, Bob."

Bob ignored Will's praise. "No, he adds more land to what he owns. Now he probably wants to get hold of my property." His face grew stern, and his eyes narrowed. "I've a good mind to paste him a couple of good ones right now."

"Hold on, Pard," Will said. Will called Bob "pard" only when it seemed he was about to go off on a tangent from his normal attitude. "Quennel won't admit nothing. From his World War I record, we know he's brave. Taking a bullet in the leg while capturing a trio of Huns proved that. We're going to have to prove him a liar 'cause he won't admit nothing."

Bob brightened. "Thanks for being a friend. Let's head for the hills, Will. I'll prove myself innocent and we'll rescue Richard, too."

"Finding Richard will be like locatin' a raindrop in a river."

"Very good," Bob said. "There's a bit of the poet inside you after all."

Shoulder to shoulder, they left the church and headed for the hills.

Bob admitted to himself while they walked along that Will was right. He might escape the law in the wilderness, but he needed all the help he could muster to prove his innocence. Could he drag his friends into his

Ed Pahnke

troubles? He looked at Will. Where else would he look for help? Toppling Gil Quennel and John King and rescuing Richard King seemed all but impossible.

What the hell, you never know what you can do until you try.

CHAPTER FOUR
THE PITFALLS OF A DETOUR

His spirits high, Bob began the three-mile hike to the Manitou hills. He was even able to joke about his wedding. "This is the longest wedding march in history. Marian may be marching for months before she reaches me." His face grew dark and his smile vanished, but reappeared as brightly a moment later.

Cross-country on foot usually presented few problems to seasoned outdoorsmen. Both Bob and Will had spent much of their lives in forest and field, but in proper clothing, not in suits and dress shoes.

"I'd never agreed to this if I thought I'd be tramping through the bush in my Sunday suit. Damn, these shoes pinch my feet. I bought 'em for sitting, not walking."

Whenever Bob looked back, he saw Will scuffing along, head down. If a stone or a twig lay in his path, he gave it a kick.

A few steps in front of Will, Bob saw one stone hurtle past him. When something hit him, he turned on his heel.

"Did you hit me with something?"

"A stick. I kicked too hard. Sorry."

"I think you should walk ahead. A man as spleenful as you is likely to burst over the trail. I wouldn't want to miss it."

Will growled and said, "I'm serious, Bob."

"How could I think otherwise. I believe I've thought of a way to get a spring in your step and a - if you'll pardon the expression - smile on your lips."

Will and Bob stopped. They faced each other. "Speak up and stop smirking," Will said. An exaggerated scowl wrinkled his forehead.

"I say we go home to pick up boots, clothing, and weapons, not much, but things fit for outdoors' living."

"What are we waiting for?" Will almost smiled. "Let's head north."

When the two grimy hikers saw Bob's log home, they stopped. His home was located on the outskirts of Carver, a village named for Jonathan Carver. Being close to Carver, his house was hooked up to electricity and telephone. Beyond the village limits, kerosene lamps lit the houses.

From a brushy knoll fifty yards from the lodge. Bob studied the landscape. The dimness of twilight slowly gave way to night. Yet no lights illuminated the buildings.

Already, Bob missed his home, his home since childhood.

Measuring ninety feet by thirty feet, the massive lodge sat on a fieldstone foundation. Peeled white pine logs rose two stories high. Numerous casement windows checkered the log walls, and cedar shake shingles crowned the precipitous roof.

The lodge had been built when the supply of white pine seemed infinite in the neighboring virgin forests, a time when everybody grew prosperous in the timber trade. But in the same way that man's greed had eliminated the passenger pigeon and decimated the bison, he ravaged the white pine. Cutover land exceeded wooded land in the early 1900's. Few foresaw the forest's demise, but those that did planned for the time by maintaining wood lots prior to 1910. Among these were the Brunets, the Quennels, and the Kings in Gamwell County, Wisconsin.

Even before the forest crop law was enacted in 1927, spindly alders and sturdy popples, the local name for aspen, had spread over many of the abandoned farms and vast cut over scars.

By 1932 there was almost as much wooded land as there was cutover land in Gamwell County. There was also economic depression that pressed upon the citizens. Many of the hardy farmers who had survived the 1920's in the county were overwhelmed by the 1930's. They fought, but it was like punching air. Frustrated and disheartened, they abandoned their homes.

To the many people who stayed, a final blow to their hopes came on June 1, 1932. Someone kidnapped Richard King, the local banker and their friend, and held him for an astronomical ransom of fifty thousand dollars. Instead of a benevolent banker, they had to turn to a spiteful one, Richard's brother, John.

Ed Pahnke

The day he gained control of the bank, John King began calling loans. With one hand, he grabbed a property; with the other he sold it to Quennel for pennies on the dollar value of an acre. Many of the local citizens wondered why Quennel wanted so much land. Was he not already the owner of more land than anyone else in the county?

Quennel's sister, Grace, opposed her brother's conduct. She invested her small inheritance in a Building and Loan in Langston, and ran the business fairly. But because of the small size of the operation, it had little if any impact on local conditions.

When John King spoke of his actions, he claimed he was protecting the interests of the bank. He continued foreclosing until the Controller of the Currency declared a moratorium on first mortgage foreclosures in August of 1932. Then John King's land-grab methods became more devious.

Bob remained silent.

"Ain't we going in?" Will whispered.

"That's why we're here, but let's look at this from all angles. Things seem quiet enough, maybe too quiet. I say we keep to the cover and circle the house, in case of an ambush," Bob said.

"We'd better move now, or it'll be too damn dark soon."

The two men began the tortuous route around the lodge. Taking advantage of every tree, shrub, and hillock, they worked their way to the north side and the dirt road.

Will brought his arm up against Bob's chest. They stopped. He pointed to a hulking shadow crouched by a fence post. "What do we do? Run?"

Northern Knights

Bob motioned forward. They inched their way ahead.

"Colt," Bob whispered and put out his hand. With the other hand, he scooped up a stone and sailed it onto the dirt road.

The shadow wheeled around. Bob rushed toward the shadow. "Keep your voice down. Who are you?"

"It's me, Bob, Mike Rood."

Handshakes followed.

In hushed tones, Reverend Mike explained, "Alice listened in on a phone call her father received. Can you imagine folks having two telephones? Anyway, it was Joe Worman. He told Sheriff Blue that you'd be coming back home for clothes. The sheriff stationed two deputies in your home to capture you."

"Worman? Are you sure? That son of a..." Bob said. Will and Mike stared at Bob. "Sorry, Mike. I trusted him. He's no floater. He's worked for me for five years, and I've known him since high school. Could Quennel have him on his payroll, too?"

Bob's face became livid as his anger mounted. "This won't stop us. We're going to get what we came for. Here's the plan."

Shedding scant light, a sliver of a new moon hung in the sky. Wind rustled through tree branches. As silent as shadows of clouds passing over the earth, Bob and Will approached the lodge. Once alongside the building, they edged toward the cellar door. They peered in every direction at once, but they didn't coordinate their steps. Bob stopped. Will didn't. The resultant scuffle brought Bob's Airedale, Rex, to the scene. The dog wagged a greeting to his master with his stubby tail. When it appeared he would bark. Bob grabbed Rex's muzzle to silence him and motioned him to lie down.

Bob eased the door open, lifting its weight to keep the hinges from creaking. When one did creak, nothing happened and seemingly nobody inside was alerted. Bob propped the heavy plank door against the log wall. The men felt their way down into the blackness. Once on the floor, they picked their way through the clutter of canned goods and tools, but every object seemed to be aimed at their toes or knees. Bumps and bruises did little to improve their dispositions.

They muttered curses under their breaths. Bob's meandering course led him to the bottom step leading to the first floor.

"I found the steps," Bob whispered. "Or rather my shin found them. Damn that hurts."

They removed their shoes before climbing the steps on tiptoes. Reaching the door, Bob slid his hand over it until he touched the doorknob. Cautiously, he turned the knob with his left hand. He squeezed Quennel's Colt revolver with his right hand and nudged the door with his shoulder. It swung open, and the men lurched out of the pitch dark.

Without an inkling as to the whereabouts of the deputies, Bob stopped. He homed in on the sound of voices coming from the front room. Walking in their stocking feet, they swiftly approached Sheriff Blue's deputies.

"This waitin' gets on my nerves," one man said. The bass whisper sounded as though it came from a tunnel.

In answer, the other man said, "Waiting here beats waiting outdoors. Remember, the sheriff wants Brunet alive, if possible. Do you see anything?"

"I see your head, but I want to see your hands," Bob said. "Raise them."

Bob and Will walked into the front room.

"Who are you?"

"I'm the home owner, and I have a Colt pointed at your bulky body."

"My hands are up." His hands were quicker than his words.

"Mine too. How'd you know we were here?"

"I heard you talking. Stand up. Will, get their guns and belts."

Will unbuckled their belts and threw their guns, belts, and holsters onto a plaid couch.

"I expect honest answers," Bob said. "Where's that back stabbing Joe Worman? I've got a grudge to settle with him. I'm going to give him one chance to leave the county, alive." He wondered if he could actually shoot a person.

"He's in his room," the gravel voiced deputy said.

"His room? He doesn't live in my home."

"What are we goin' to do with this pair of deuces?" Will asked.

"Lock 'em in the closet. We're locking up more folks than a jailer today. This time I know there's a key."

Quickly, Will herded the two deputies into the front hall closet and locked the door.

At the same time, Bob bolted up the stairs to the bedrooms. He reached his room, and Colt in hand, he burst inside. His gaze fastened on the brass bed next to an oak commode. A smell of stale cigar smoke hung in the room, and a Tiffany lamp sitting on the commode glowed brightly.

"Get up, Joe," Bob said waving the Colt .45. "I want you standing tall with your hands held high."

"Bob! How the hell did you get in here?"

"I'm not in the mood to answer questions, but I'll tell you this. Come on in, Will. Where was I? Oh, yeah. I'll tell you this. You'd better get out of Gamwell County, and hope that it's far enough away, so I never see again. Next time I see you, wherever it is, God forgive me, I shoot to kill. Tie him to a chair, and don't be gentle with the honyock."

Will tied Worman to a ladder-back chair with the rope he had brought.

Bob gathered clothes, boots, a razor, and ammunition, and stuffed them into a packsack. He chose a twelve gage double-barreled shotgun from his gun cabinet, barely glancing at the dozen shooting trophies he'd been awarded over the years. They were arranged on top of the cabinet.

His first choice would have been a lever-action rifle, but he needed a dual-purpose gun for hunting in heavy brush. With the Stevens Riverside, he was ready for buck or bird, depending on the load. The shotgun had been in the family since he was a boy. He also took a twenty-two caliber High Standard pistol that Marian had bought for him and stuck it in his belt. The pistol had a ten shot clip and would be useful for either self-defense or pot hunting in the forest.

Will turned to leave to pack some of his clothes when finished tying Worman.

"Stop in the basement to pick up our shoes," Bob said while putting a gray, slouch hat on his head. He had felt almost undressed without a hat. "Get some tools too." After a pause, he added, "Please. And hurry."

Bob didn't want to give Joe Worman or the deputies a hint that he and Will were heading for the Manitou Hills. He and Will wouldn't change clothes until Mike Rood left them in the wilderness. All that Worman could say for certain was that Bob and Will were wearing suits.

Turning to Worman, Bob said, "Here's Quennel's revolver." He threw it onto the bed. "Give it to him on your way out of the county. I wouldn't want him to think I stole it. I don't make idle threats. So, good-by, Joe. I'm sorry I ever met you."

"Listen to me, Bob," Worman said. "I wanted to be someone. The only times we ever talked I done something wrong or you were giving me orders. I needed more than that. After all, we've known each other since high school. I thought more was coming to me. I…"

"I recognized you were doing your share, and I trusted you. We talked plenty, but you were only receptive when I praised you. Did you try to get special treatment because we were friends? We all had to work together to make good. I could never trust you again."

Will came into the room. "Are you ready?" he asked Bob while handing him his dress shoes. "When do we, change? These shoes ain't comfortable."

"As soon as we get where we're going." Bob tugged the shoes on to his feet while he talked.

Will nodded.

Ed Pahnke

Without further comment, Bob and Will tramped outside. In front of the house, Rex danced about and wagged his tail.

"Looks like you got another volunteer, Bob," Will said. "He's a dandy hunter."

At the word "hunter," Rex's ears stood up and he romped about again.

While they stood on the dirt road in front of the lodge, Reverend Mike Rood pulled up beside the trio in his Model "T".

Before joining him in his automobile, Bob looked wistfully back at his home. When would he be able to live there like a normal human being? He frowned. He knew the road back would be rough, winding, and all up hill.

"Hop in, fellows," Mike said. "What do you say, Rex?"

Rex scampered to Mike's side. Mike scratched Rex behind his ears.

"If the pup says a word, we can sell him for plenty," Will said.

Mike shook his head and smiled. Bob and Will joined Rex inside the automobile.

"Do you think you can take care of Rex for a while, Mike?" Bob asked. "We're about to start a dangerous game, and we've got to travel light."

Will looked at Bob, then at Mike.

Mike nodded. "I know you love Rex, but you're doing the best thing for him. Sure, I'll take him for a while."

Mike shifted into first gear, and they chugged off toward the Manitou Hills three miles away.

CHAPTER FIVE
MEN OF THE MANITOU HILLS

In three miles, the rolling countryside changed into the wooded, craggy Manitou Hills. Though he lived close enough to the hills to see them daily, Bob seldom visited the region, but he had been raised in the wilderness and knew how to survive. To thrive in the hills, his sense of hearing, sight, and smell would need to be sharp. He reflected upon what he expected the hills to hold in store.

The thirty square miles of wild woodlands were largely without roads. To traverse the wilderness, a rover depended upon a network of game trails that wound about the steep, tree covered hills. The region was one of swift streams such as Quartz Creek and small lakes such as Bear Claw Lake.

The sound of the great forest was wind. On stormy nights, wind moaned through the trees. On wintry days, wind rattled naked tree branches. On bright spring days, wind danced in the treetops. Wind also carried the sweet odor of wildflowers abroad. On lowering days, the smell of moisture visited the nostrils. When the sky was azure blue, the piquant scent of evergreens often filled the air.

Formerly a region of white pine forest, the rugged hills had made lumbering difficult. Some stands of white pine escaped the nineteenth century timber pirates. After lumberjacks had left clean cutover scars, lumber barons coaxed farmers to buy cheap, cutover land. Few of those farms survived into the twentieth century. Once earth had healed herself, trees grew in again, blanketing the countryside.

At one time, a logging railroad had snaked its way through the hills. In scattered places in the hills, a few rotted ties and rusty spikes could still be found attesting to the railroad's presence. This land would be Bob's and Will's home.

After being bumped and jolted over dusty roads for three miles, Bob and Will gladly scrambled from Mike's Model T. They shook hands. Rex extended a paw, and Bob shook it. Will declined the gesture. Mike turned the flivver about while Bob and Will waved good-by.

When the chugging and snorting of the model T had died away into a wall of lengthening black shadows, Bob and Will shouldered their packs. They looked at each other as if to ask, "Where to now?" Did they have a choice? In front of them, a narrow path cut through the bush leading to who knew where; and behind them, the law puffed and snorted trying to pick up their scent. Before they could lift a foot, however, they heard hoof beats. Not a steady lope, it was the clump, clump of a draft horse.

"What the hell?" Will peered around.

Bob strained his eyes looking along the shadowy road. Lights from two lanterns came into view, dancing about crazily. A rattling of harness chains accompanied the clop of hooves along with a clattering that sounded like pans banging together. The silhouettes of a horse and wagon came into view. A sturdy but old chestnut drew the wagon. The blaze on its forehead looked as grizzled as the shaggy mane and moustache of the driver.

Bob and Will could barely make out the sign painted on the side of the red rig: "Calvin Little, Esq. General Merchandise." From backcountry travel, the spokes of the wheels were dusty yellow color.

"This is our first test, Will. We're outlaws, so we should act like outlaws."

"You don't mean rob that geezer? Why, hell, Bob, I don't know nothing about robbing folks."

"I don't either, but when we went to school, we learned by practicing. That peddler won't give us any trouble. When I wave this shotgun about, he'll be quaking in his boots."

After loading his shotgun and cocking the hammers, Bob strode to the center of the road and signaled the peddler to stop.

"Good evening. Are you Mr. Little?" Bob asked.

"Little is my moniker but not my size," the peddler said. He swung himself off the board seat onto a step. With an agility that belied his size and age, he jumped to the ground and faced Bob and Will.

The burly fellow stuck out his baseball glove sized hand. The smile that lit his face etched two dimples onto his ruddy cheeks.

"Evening, fellow vagabonds," he said while shaking their hands vigorously. "Are you interested in purchasing some of my goods?"

As tall as Bob and as broad as Will, Cal Little loosened a catch and the hinged wooden side panel dropped down, revealing an assortment of canned goods and dry goods.

"We can use all of these things," Bob said.

The smile on the peddler's face became so broad that it pushed up his cheek and about closed his eyes. "I hope you'll leave some stock for my next customer. You start picking and I'll start adding up."

"No need to trouble yourself adding anything up. We don't intend to pay." Bob's smile broadened as a puzzled expression replaced the grin on Cal's face. "We'll take everything including your horse and wagon."

Bob pointed the double barrel shotgun at the peddler. "This twelve gauge isn't loaded with bird shot," Bob said.

"Is it a deer load?" Calvin Little asked.

Bob chuckled to himself. He couldn't resist. He said, "I like it, but I wouldn't say it's a dear load."

"Come on, Bob," Will said. "Get down to business, no nonsense."

His brow furrowed, the peddler looked first at Bob then at Will. When no explanation was given, he said, "So you two are road agents preying on honest tradesmen. Cowards at that if you need a shotgun, however loaded, to subdue an ol' man."

"Don't let it be said I don't believe in fair play," Bob said. Easing the hammers forward, he placed the shotgun on top of his pack and then removed his jacket. "I'll give this bumpkin a drubbing, and we'll be on our way with his wagon and trade goods."

"Those are bold words for such a puny rascal," Cal said.

"Our muscles are packed solid," Will said. A sneer curled his lips.

"Is that true above the neck too?" Cal said. "I wouldn't want to damage those muscles." He slipped off his brown, wool cardigan.

Bob rolled up his sleeves. "We've no such worry about damaging anything important above your neck. Stand back, Will. I'll take care of this fellow."

He danced about the peddler jabbing and feinting in the best pugilistic style. Suddenly he rushed Cal. In response, the peddler straight-armed Bob. The punch launched him off his feet. He tumbled backward and landed on his butt in the road, sending up a small cloud of dust.

More embarrassed than hurt, Bob scrambled to his feet. He said, "You have a way with your fists, peddler. Now that you've proved you're not all hot air, I'll be more wary."

"Will, shall I show this lout the fine points of fisticuffs?" He turned his full attention to the peddler. "If you wonder how I got this broken nose, I was a sparring partner for Jack Sharkey."

"I learned to defend myself when I was deputy sheriff in Chester County," Cal said. "I'm on the ballot in Gamwell County for sheriff as an independent."

After Bob's stab at psychological warfare failed, he danced and jabbed again, moving around the larger man. He scoffed at anybody's chances to win on his own in an election. After a jab, he lashed out with a straight right that caught the peddler on his square jaw. Cal rocked back and shook his head.

Bob's reaction was more pronounced. He smiled and rubbed his knuckles. "What the hell is your jaw made of, granite?"

"Your fists are fast, stranger. That punch stung."

"I'd rather have you a friend than a foe, Cal. If I could vote, I'd vote for you against Roland Blue. Unfortunately, the law considers me an outlaw. I'm Bob Brunet, and my friend here, is Will Scathlock. I'm hoping to organize a group of men who are tired of John King and Gil Quennel stepping on them. Would you consider throwing in with us?"

"Most anybody in Gamwell County will rally round your banner to overthrow that band of rascals," Cal said. "You can depend on me to add my muscle to the cause. I can offer some of my goods, too, but I can't afford much."

Shaking Cal's hand, Bob said, "I think you'll be most helpful if you continue to sell your goods. You don't want to hurt what chances you have of getting elected by associating with outlaws. You can be our eyes in town, and keep us informed about people and events throughout the county."

"You want me to be a spy like Nightshade O'Neil in the pulps?" Cal said.

"Exactly, but no mask." A smile lit Bob's face. "They'll never suspect a person bigger than life right in front of their eyes, especially if he's running for sheriff. But for now, we need a place to base our operations."

"A camp," Will said. He yawned. "A safe place to lay our heads down and sleep."

"I know the perfect place, a glade deep in the bush. I found it when I was out looking for a likely trout stream." While talking, Cal closed the panel on the side of the wagon. "Jump aboard. Thunder will take us to a path leading there."

He climbed onto the wagon seat and held out his hands to pull Bob and Will aboard on each side of him.

They took a long look at the graying chestnut before throwing their goods onto the wagon roof and clambering alongside Cal. Thunder didn't seem an appropriate name for the clumsy gelding.

"How did you come up with the name Thunder for your horse?" Will asked.

Cal laughed. "Usually I don't tell the story when Thunder's nearby. I think it embarrasses him, but I'll satisfy your curiosity.

"When he was a young colt, he had a problem." His voice sunk to a whisper. "He had a gas problem, very loud farts. So loud, in fact, we thought of thunder, so we called him Thunder."

Will and Bob looked at the big horse. His ears lay back on his head, and he scraped the ground with his hoof. Was he eager to get started, or did he resent Cal's story?

Cal flicked the reins. "Up Thunder."

Thunder jerked forward. He dug his hoofs into the dirt and broke into a canter. The wagon shook. Wooden boards squeaked against each other. Pans rattled. Cans tumbled.

"Easy, Thunder. Slow down."

Northern Knights

Cal pulled back on the reins. Thunder shook his head but continued.

Cal turned to Bob. "I should never've told you that story." Cal's eyeballs bounced in their sockets, and his words bounced with them. Once again, Cal pulled back on the reins. Thunder slackened his pace to a walk. He stopped, looked back at the trio behind him and whinnied.

"There's a trail, I think," Will said.

"You're right," Cal said. "That's where it begins."

The glow of the lanterns revealed a path partially hidden by a bank of alders that choked either side of the rutted dirt road. The path had probably been trod by wild animals and wild Indians alike. It appeared to point to a notch between two barely visible distant hills.

Bob and Will jumped down and hobbled about trying to work out the kinks.

Cal passed down guns, pack sacks, and blankets made of rabbit skins woven together to Will and Bob. They quickly exchanged stiff dress shoes for heavy oil tanned moccasin style boots, and suits for outdoor clothing.

"Maybe you can sell our shoes and suits, Cal. We won't need them in the bush," Bob said. "It'll be impossible to find our way to that glade tonight, though."

Pushed by a brisk wind, clouds raced by a sliver of moon, alternately hiding and revealing it.

"Sleep here," Cal said. "Spread your blankets under the wagon. Have breakfast with me, and travel refreshed in the morning, after I've given you directions to the glade."

Bob lay under the wagon thinking about Joe Worman. How could someone he knew and trusted betray him? Mercenaries might fight for King and Quennel while the money streamed to them, but Bob counted on belief in a lawful cause for his support. People throughout the county wanted a change, but he had to find them and point them toward a common goal. Where would he find them in the deep forest? Maybe they'd find him, like Cal did.

He turned on his side and fell asleep.

CHAPTER SIX
A HOME AWAY FROM HOME

Packsacks slung over their backs with straps pressing against their foreheads, Bob and Will pushed along the forest path. Bob shifted his pack about, but he found no comfortable way to carry it. The morning sun edged over the horizon. Somewhere ahead of them lay the hidden glade about which Cal had told them.

Once past the alders, they skirted a tamarack swamp. On the upland side of the swamp, a scattering of white pine vied for space with masses of birch and popple. Rays of sun filtered through a mixture of yellow and green leaves and evaporated the dew. By the time they had bumped into a wall of wild roses, the sun blazed on their gray, felt slouch hats. Wild roses had settled in the sunny valley and climbed hills on either side. Undoubtedly there were enough rose hips clinging to the branches to produce a hundred or more jars of jam.

First Bob, then Will wiped his forehead with his sleeve. They took off and slung their blue-black mackinaws over their shoulders. Bob wore a gray wool shirt and faded blue corduroys. Will wore a red flannel shirt and wide cut black, wool trousers.

"Where the hell did the trail disappear to?" Will asked.

"There it is," Bob said, pointing. "See it. Animals must tunnel through. The trail's dead ahead."

The men crouched and saw the trail dive into the valley beyond a decayed deadfall.

"I think we can bend down and get through," Bob said, crouching. "Think of it this way, Will. The more obstacles we bump into, the harder it will be for anyone else to find us."

"My back don't see things that way."

Ducking, they plowed through. Once beyond the natural hedge, the trail continued between two craggy hills. Stands of ancient white pine stood sentinel on either side of them.

Will stopped and studied the trees for a moment. "How'd those old fellows escape the axe?"

"With so many acres of white pine, why wrestle with the remote stands?"

Bob and Will had slowed to a trudge before they finally left the valley. When they did, a wide meadow greeted them. An old log cabin, grayed with age, squatted in the center of the glade; and next to it, a huge bull spruce dominated the clearing. No glass remained in the cabin's windows. The roof proved to be of scoop design. Straight saplings had been split length ways and hollowed out. One layer was placed trough side up; the other was placed trough side down. A long sapling was fastened trough side down over the ridge. The walls and roof looked sturdy enough.

They set about to make the cabin habitable.

"We have a visitor, Bob." Will, his hand was poised in mid air, nodded his head to indicate a man walking toward them.

For the past several hours, Will had been hammering salvaged nails into floorboards to secure them to floor joists on the porch. Bob had been shuttering windows with salvaged wood.

"Try to be friendly and nonchalant until we find out the reason for his visit."

"Me, friendly?" Will said. "Am I ever anything else?" The stony expression on his face answered his own questions. "I don't want to keep moving. Even though this place ain't much, it's shelter."

Stepping off the porch, Bob said, "Afternoon, stranger."

The diminutive man, with his sharp chin, turned up nose, and wide mouth, could have passed for a forest elf or pixy. Would he have reached five feet tall standing on his tiptoes?

"Afternoon, Sirs," he said. "My name is Nat, short for Nathaniel." He doffed his peaked deerskin cap with one hand while holding a gnarled wooden staff with the other. A maze of patches covered his overalls, and his pants legs were tucked into high-topped leather boots. A brown wool shirt and a mottled deerskin vest completed his outfit.

Without using their last names, Bob and Will introduced themselves.

"I'd never have found this glade if it hadn't been for your pounding." Bob and Will glanced at each other. "As it is, I darned near broke a leg following that stream through a canyon." He pointed to the sparkling water cutting a path through the meadow. "I hopped from rock to rock like a grasshopper to get through.

"You gentlemen plan to take up residence here?"

"It seems like a good shelter for two weary knights of the road."

"Well put, friend Bob. I would deem it an honor if you would allow me to join you."

"Why would you think I need or want anybody to join up with me?"

Will plopped the head of the hammer he was holding into the palm of one hand. His eyes narrowed, he measured the distance between himself and the elfin man.

Oblivious to Will's combative vibrations, Nat said, "Friends tell friends. One of the men living near the hills was at the church. Now, many of the dispossessed in the great forest know Bob Brunet escaped from Sheriff Blue and Gil Quennel yesterday. An unjust accusation has made you one of us. Together, perhaps, we may all get what we strive for."

"What makes you think I'm this Brunet fellow?"

"I worked for you once. Joe Worman bossed our crew."

"How do you know I'm not a thief? Why should I trust a loose tongue like you?"

Will was about to swing on the little man, but Bob held his right arm in front of Will.

"Not loose tongue but honest speech. We know about you and the help you extended to many in the past, and we don't believe you're a thief. There are about twenty of us in camps scattered throughout the great forest of the Manitou. Our hands are extended to you in friendship."

Northern Knights

He thrust his hand toward Bob, who took it in his. He gave it a hardy handshake, as did somber Will.

"Would you like to meet the men?" Nat asked.

Bob saw a readymade brigade of outlaws. The last vestige of his caution vanished. Nat seemed open and frank. In his mind's eye, he saw a jolly troop of musketeers, all for one, and one for all. Also he thought of Benjamin Franklin's words, "Yes, we must, indeed, all hang together, or, most assuredly, we shall all hang separately."

All these men needed was a resourceful, optimistic leader. If he were that leader, Gamwell County might yet be free of John King, Roland Blue, and Gil Quennel.

"How soon can you round them up to meet here, Nat?"

"I'll pass the word down the line this afternoon and give them directions to find this place. They'll be here tomorrow morning."

Morning fog enveloped the seventeen men gathered in the forest meadow. The rays of sun filtering through white pines, popples, and birches dappled shadows across their faces. On that early September morning, a few round, yellow leaves floated down from trees to land in the middle of the gathering.

Many of the men were dressed in patched, faded overalls; wide brimmed, black slouch hats; and work soiled, denim coats. Directed by Nat, they had straggled in from camps scattered throughout the Manitou Hills. Some arrived around dusk the previous day, and some arrived earlier that same morning.

While trudging along any one of two trails that ended in the glade, they likely had one question in their minds. Can Bob Brunet help us to get our homes and farms back? All veteran woodsmen, they noted where deer had bedded down, where grouse took flight, and where squirrels chattered. Their noses had picked up the aroma of evergreens and of damp grasses. Sure footed in their brogan shoes, they had jumped over trickles of water or waded through clear, gurgling streams.

Upon arriving in the glade, they had congregated in small groups and waited for Bob to speak to them.

Bob waited too. He stood in the meadow talking with Will. As though on command, Bob turned on his heel. He walked a couple of paces before bounding onto the trunk of a wind fallen tree.

"Men," he shouted. "Gather 'round."

They squinted up at Bob, their faces sun wrinkled, their beards stubbly.

"All here are woodsmen by choice or by necessity. We've been thrown off our land by the same ruthless band of pirates, whose names stick in our throats. We all have one aim, to return to our homes.

"I have another goal. I have been accused of theft by Gil Quennel."

"Damn him!" the crowd howled. They had a common enemy. Bob raised his hand to still the commotion.

He continued, "I am innocent, but I need your help, too. If we work together, we can - we will overthrow that gang of scoundrels. Finding and rescuing Richard King will help all of us."

"That wild Indian, Leo Long Mane, has got Richard King hid away somewhere," A voice yelled from the throng.

"So I've read in the Vinette Weekly Journal. John King is his accuser, and all of you know how much faith we put in his words. We must work outside the law to find the truth. If Leo Long Mane is innocent, he has nothing to fear from us. Only the guilty must fear us. There's strength in numbers; would you like to make this glade your home?"

"Yes! We're with you, Bob," they said in one voice.

"Will found dry caves in the cliff on the other side of the stream," Bob said. "We have a cabin, and we'll build other log shelters to see us through the winter, if that's what it takes.

"Pack up your belongings. Bring along food if you have any. The forest will supply wild game. Our enemies and my friends will supply any other needs. This glade will be a home for the lost who wish to find justice.

"We need something to distinguish us from other folks, a kind of uniform to identify us one to another in troubled times."

From the ranks, Nat said, "Three dozen forest-green Filson cruisers are impounded at the railroad station in Vinette. The owners are broke. The railroad's stuck with the coats and wants sixty bucks."

"Perfect," Bob said. "We'll need money to make them an offer. I say we raid John King's bank. It's time he served the community."

Ed Pahnke

A murmur of agreement quickly grew to a din. Faces that had begun the meeting with bleak, hopeless expressions held smiles after Bob finished speaking.

"I'll have someone watch the bank, but this won't be stealing. I have an account at the bank, at least I had money there, three hundred and some odd dollars, all I have.

"Will, Nat, let's make plans to get the money and provisions for the men. Follow me to the cabin."

CHAPTER SEVEN
THE OLD WOLF

Three days after the first gathering of Bob's brigade, Cal strode into a bustling encampment. Bob and Will looked up from a fire where a pig was turning on a spit. Several men recognized the peddler and waved.

After a round of handshakes, Bob, Will, and Cal trooped to the log cabin. Once inside, Bob asked, "What news do you have from town?"

"The hike here takes a lot out of a man." Cal mopped his forehead with a red kerchief and smiled, the relieved kind of smile reserved for a job well done. His teeth were discolored from years of pipe smoking, and a briar, smelling of old tobacco ash, bulged from his vest pocket.

"The best time for you to visit the bank is right after one o'clock. The town gets deserted," Cal said. "People usually take care of their in town business in the morning.

"Within an ace of being like us. Eh, Bob?" Will interrupted. "We never went into town in the afternoon neither. Why do you think that is?"

"Anything else you want to add, or can I continue?"

Will looked sheepish and kept his mouth closed.

"Park in front of the bank."

"Park?" Bob said. "We haven't got an automobile or wagon to park."

"Borrow a flivver. Don't attempt anything on foot."

"I suppose we can arrange that."

"You and Will sure do butt in on a fellow. As I was saying. Some of the employees eat lunch at the Palace Restaurant. Even John King is out. He goes home for lunch at one."

"Thanks, Cal. No reason to delay. Nat, Will, and I will make a withdrawal tomorrow or the day after."

"Nat?" Will asked. "Can we trust him?"

"Am I a good judge of character?" Bob said.

"You think everybody is good until I put you wise."

"You keep watch on him then," Bob said and smiled. "I stand by my decision."

Cal edged toward the door. He cleared his throat to gain Bob's attention, then said, "I have to get back to my wagon. Business calls."

Bob and Will approached Cal. He reached out both hands and grasped Bob's and Will's hands before leaving. They watched from the doorway when he vanished through a wall of trees that surrounded the glade.

Bob turned to Will. "Do you have any ideas where we can pick up an automobile?"

Will frowned. "I thought you knew of a place, the way you spoke up when Cal mentioned an automobile.

Bob scratched his head. "Where's the closest civilization?"

"Chick's Oakwood Tavern, I suppose."

Arriving about five in the evening, Bob and Will were weary after a five hour hike. The sun had begun to set red, and a chill glow cast long shadows over the tavern.

Constructed of white pine, Chick's Oakwood Tavern rose two stories. Cedar shake shingles topped the roof, while a stone chimney protruded through the center of the roof. Next to the tavern, an ancient grove of white oaks gave the tavern its name. They marked an indistinct boundary between boreal forests and the deciduous woodlands to the south. The oaks usually produced a bumper crop of acorns for deer, grouse, and squirrels. Older than any trees in the nearby forest, the oaks had probably endured primeval fires. Later, they escaped lumberjacks who sought white pine. While the rest of the forest renewed, the oaks remained steadfast.

"I'm tired and hungry," Will said, never shy about grumbling.

"This time of year, they're probably crying for business," Bob said. "We should get a room, food, and good service, to boot."

"I hope they don't have an Injun cook," Will said.

"As long as the food is good, what does it matter?"

"It's that they can't cook plain American food."

"Where did you get that notion?" Bob said.

Ed Pahnke

"I was over to Sawyer County a couple of years back. You know there's lots of Injuns there. They was trying to sell wild rice. I was thinking about buying a supply. We was eating in one of their lodges. I asked for apple pie. Nobody knew how to make one. They had no apples either."

"How was the food otherwise?"

"I was hungry. I was ready to eat anything."

Bob and Will had been standing in front of the lodge. Matched gray geldings were hitched to a green buckboard that stood in the parking lot. The buckboard had probably been built before the turn of the century, but replacement parts and pride in the wagon had kept it looking new. There was no other sign of life at the tavern.

Will walked up the weathered wooden steps, and pushed open the heavy plank door. It swung easily. The smell of dry pine permeated the room and refreshed Bob's nostrils. Copper chandeliers fueled by kerosene provided light in the huge room. Pine posts supported the second floor balcony. The posts, the floor, and the walls weren't stained. They remained their natural color under coats of varnish.

A long mahogany bar stood at the far end of the dining room. Chick, a short blond man, yawned behind the bar. A lone customer bent his sinewy six-foot frame over the bar with a stein of lager clutched in his sun-bronzed hands. His black slouch hat lay on the bar next to him.

"Ain't that Arno Ingram?" Will asked.

"That's Arno all right. He's a lone wolf if there ever was one. Some folks say he'd rather fight than farm, but I've found him to be friendly if not sociable. He must be every day of sixty, but he doesn't look it. He's got a farm nearby, doesn't he?"

"Maybe he can help us, if it's one of his good days," Will said.

"It's worth a try."

The two men strode over to where Arno stood.

"Afternoon, Arno," Bob said.

Arno Ingram looked up and smiled through his iron gray mustache. His eyes were the deep blue of a gas flame.

"Why, Bob Brunet. And Will Scathlock, too. Good to see you boys again. I heard you was in a peck o' trouble."

He wrung their hands heartily while he spoke. His hands were hard as walnut burls.

"I'm trying to get out of trouble. I never stole in my life, but Quennel's got me in hiding."

"Seems John King and Gil Quennel has got the county by the throat, and they're squeezing hard," Arno said. "I'm in the midst of harvesting on my farm, but I needed to get away. My tongue's been hollering for beer, but there ain't many places where a fellow can get a stein. Care to join me?"

"Thanks." Bob smiled. "I'd be proud to join you."

"Likewise," Will said.

Chick filled two more steins.

After taking a healthy draft, Bob said, "I wonder if you could help us? We have to get hold of an automobile, to conduct some business."

"I can't help you. I don't even drive, but I have a horse and wagon out front. You can use them."

Bob took a sip of beer. Than he said, "Do you know anybody hereabouts with an automobile?"

Arno scratched the back of his neck. A smile formed slowly on his lips. "You boys is outlaws anyways, and you know me. I don't give a damn. John King owns the farm next door to me. He's never there. A couple o' hired hands works the place. Sons o' bitches if there ever was ones. King's farm must be a section. I've got only a hundred and twenty acres, but they keep sending cattle onto my fields. I found fences cut. I cussed that pair left and right, and they laughed.

"One day a white face was eating oats in one of my fields. I shot it and butchered it. They yelled, and I smiled. They yelled and cussed all the louder. They threatened to have John King foreclose my mortgage, but I laughed and told 'em I owned my farm free and clear. They fumed and stomped off my property. They keep their livestock off my land now, but I find cut fences.

"Now here's the point o' my story. They got an automobile. You boys can drive, and you need an automobile. I'll help you get it. I know the lay o' the land. We'll have a good old time. How about it?" Arno grinned.

"Hell, yes," Will said and took a long swallow of beer.

Will hadn't waited for Bob's answer. Bob wasn't thief, but it would be justice of a sort.

"Here's my hand on the deal," Bob said. "Can we get the automobile tonight?"

"How about food first?" Will said.

"You boys haven't ate good food till you sat at my table. My wife's as good a cook as there is, and I should be heading on home now. Join me."

"We can't burst into your house without warning your wife," Bob said.

"Hell, she'll be glad for the company. I suspect she's tired of seeing just me." He added, "She made apple pie."

"Lets go, Bob," Will tugged Bob's sleeve.

"We accept your invitation, Arno," Bob said. "Thanks."

Surrounded by a pine windbreak, the farmstead looked as though it had been built at the turn of the century and left to weather since then. Not a speck of paint clung to the silver gray walls. Lantern light showed through sparkling glass windows, probably kept sparkling by Truda Ingram. Wooden shutters were hooked back against the walls.

Before leaving to tend to his horses, Arno led Bob and Will into the house. Truda Ingram greeted them with open arms and seated them before Arno returned.

After supper, Bob and Will, led by Arno, marched off to John King's farm. A set of white, painted buildings loomed in the moonlight. John King's farm looked as though it had received a coat of paint that very day.

Arno whispered, "I've been here before without an invitation. They keep the automobile in the barn. I seen it there when I come here to raise hell about my fences. I took a couple of swings at one of 'em, but the other one pointed a shotgun at me. That was last week, and I been fuming ever since." He smiled and rubbed his hands together. A single word escaped from his mouth, "Revenge."

"We'd best put masks over our faces," Bob said. "If any of us is recognized, our business venture could fail. You don't want to be recognized do you, Arno?"

"We kill 'em and bury 'em if they recognize us. Simple," Arno said.

Bob looked at Arno to see if there was any glimmer of humor in his remarks, and the look convinced him that Arno was not a reluctant outlaw. He relished a ruckus. His reputation as a scrapper, a man who would fight to the death, was genuine

Bob felt cold and clammy. "We want to avoid bloodshed," he said.

Arno smiled as though to say he pitied Bob's weakness. "You want the automobile, and I say let's get it, no buck fever. I'll keep watch for those bastards or their dog, looks like a young malamute."

Bob and Will ran shoulder to shoulder across the farmyard. The full moon threw their shadows ahead of them. Bob unfastened the wooden latch and swung the door open. Black was bright compared to the inside of the barn. Could the dog be inside?

"What was that?" Will whispered. "There it is again, kind o' like a low growl."

A shiver ran the course of Bob's body. The primal fear of wolves gripped him. Would he sense an attack by the dog, or would it be ripping away at him before he saw it?

Arno had been standing a few paces away. He crunched across the hard ground to where Will and Bob stood. "What's the hold up?"

"I think the dog's in the barn, somewhere. We thought we heard low growls," Will said.

From out of the blackness, Bob heard the sound of padded feet racing across hard ground, then panting.

"Look out!" Will screamed in a whisper.

A dusky shape with glowing eyes dashed out of the barn. Arno jumped in front of Bob and Will. The dog stopped moving, but it continued to growl softly. Opening its jaws, it rushed at Arno, and leaped at him. Arno planted his feet. He braced his hands in front of him. Just before he and the dog were about to meet, Arno reached his hands into the dog's mouth. Gripping each jaw, Arno yanked his hands apart.

The dog yelped, then was still. Arno had broken the malamute's lower jaw. It lay in shock. Arno stepped on the dog's rib cage with his full weight. Soon it stopped breathing.

"That took one hell of a lot o' guts, Arno," Will said.

Arno chuckled. "Chalk it up to good timing. Get the automobile started. I think this evens the score, and then some."

Bob felt around in the blackness until he found the automobile. He scrambled aboard.

"We have to crank it, Will."

"By 'we,' you mean me. Right?"

Will found the crank. After a few turns of the handle, the 1927 Model "T" started, but it didn't run quietly.

Ed Pahnke

"Hop in, Will."

Bob shifted gears, and the flivver rolled into the farmyard. Without being asked, Arno swung aboard. When they chugged along the road, Bob heard yells directed at them. He pushed hard on the gas pedal, and the car bounced along the lane toward the road. They had their getaway car.

CHAPTER EIGHT
THE RAID

Main Street had been paved with bricks for five years. It cut through the business section of town past King's Mercantile Bank. Bob parked the flivver in front of the bank. His hands felt cold and clammy, but he tried to act nonchalant. Tripping on the car's running board made him feel anything but nonchalant, but he brazened out the slip by thumping his friends on their backs. When the trio drew abreast of each other, they sauntered toward the bank.

Bob looked up at the building. The solid red face brick building boasted sandstone windowsills. The sills supported two large windows, which were protected by black, iron bars.

Will pushed the door open. Behind all of the fortifications, an armed guard dozed on a chair in the lobby. Dust coated the butt of his blue steel revolver. The only other employee in the bank busied himself behind the bars of a teller's cage.

Bob and Will dressed in blue-black mackinaws strolled through the doorway. Behind them, in his usual garb, came Nat. Nobody paid them any attention, so Will and Nat stationed themselves on either side of the dozing bank guard.

Bob leaned against the teller's window. "I want to make a withdrawal. Here's my withdrawal order."

He pushed the slip of paper under the bars.

"My God," the teller whispered hoarsely. His eyes bulged and his mouth dropped open. "Bob Brunet."

"Any problem?" Bob asked. He carried the twenty-two caliber semi-automatic pistol he had brought from home. It nestled in the inside pocket of his mackinaw, and he curled his fingers around the butt. Bob had never read a primer explaining what every tyro bank robber needed to know about guns, but he thought about Gil Quennel's revolver.

"No, sir. How much money was that again?"

"Three hundred and ninety-two dollars and fifty cents. Make that in ones, fives, and tens. I'm closing my account."

The teller whistled nervously while he flipped out the bills and topped the pile with a half-dollar. His prominent Adam's apple bounced up and down while he counted, and he gulped when he dropped the last bill on the counter.

Bob gathered the money into a neat pile before folding it into his pocket. "Thanks."

When Bob turned, his eyes met those of a completely wide-awake guard who recognized him. The guard's hand moved to the gun in his holster, but Nat stood next to him fingering his gnarled walking staff. With a deft move, he swung the staff across the guard's gun hand. From the other side, Will let fly a left hook that bounced off the guard's jaw. His head flopped back, then forward onto his chest.

The trio of outlaws quickly exited the bank. They hopped aboard the Model T. The grin on Bob's face threatened to break into a laugh. It had almost been too easy. He tried to start the automobile, and his euphoria ended. The balky car refused to start; a mule was less obstinate. They had not thought to leave the automobile running.

"Will, man the crank," Bob said.

"Why do I always get the tough jobs?"

"Who else works so tirelessly."

"My ass. You need a strong back is all."

Grumbling Will marched to the crank. Even after a few turns, the engine refused to start. Intent upon their task, they didn't notice a man walk up in back of their flivver.

"Need some help?" asked a deep voice. A badge shinned on his broad chest, and his cheeks dimpled with a smile.

Startled, Bob turned. He faced Sheriff Roland Blue. "Blue!"

"Brunet!"

The sheriff narrowed his eyes, his lips tightening. He grabbed at his hip for his forty-five caliber Colt revolver. Nat launched himself off the back seat. He thudded on Roland's chest but bounced off as though he had hit a stone wall.

Momentarily, Roland Blue concentrated on fending off the flying elf-sized man. Bob fumbled for the pistol in the inside pocket of his mackinaw. His foot pressed on the gas pedal. The engine turned over. Will climbed

Ed Pahnke

onto the back seat. Nat, his head still spinning, clambered aboard while Bob shifted the automobile into gear.

Sheriff Blue clamped his left hand onto a car door. While running alongside the moving Model T, he again reached for his revolver. Picking up a monkey wrench. Will swung it at Roland's hand. Blue yanked his hand from the door, lost his balance, and somersaulted onto the pavement.

Nat waved at the decked sheriff, and he said to Bob, "Head for Walt's Yard. There's a quick way out of town."

"Bastards," Blue yelled at the trio.

Standing near by, old Mrs. Girard probably made a note of the invective for future conversation openers about Bob Brunet.

Bob glanced over his shoulder. Revolver in hand, Roland scrambled into position for a quick shot. The sound echoed across the town. Roland grinned when the bullet ripped into the right rear tire. Heedless of the danger, Bob kept his foot on the gas-peddle. He quickly regretted his foolhardy behavior.

Unable to control the flivver, Bob yelled, "Jump before we hit."

They jumped, the flivver bumped off the street, and they landed in a tangled pile in the center of the street, The car crashed into the wooden loading dock at Walt's Feed and Grain. The radiator burst sending a geyser of hot water into the air. A wheel fractured from the axle. It bounced across the street and through the window of the Vinette Weekly Journal, nothing like putting a story into the laps of the press. A lone news hawk came to the window and shook his fist at Bob.

Turning, he yelled at an unseen coworker, "Kill the 'Brunet Whereabouts Unknown' headline."

By that time Roland Blue was puffing up the street. He got off another shot. It ricocheted from the Model T into the hole the loose wheel had opened up in the Journal Building's window.

"Duck!" the news hawk yelled out. He followed his own advice.

The shot had the opposite effect on Bob, Will, and Nat. They jumped to their feet. With Bob in the lead, the trio skirted the red clapboard feed and grain building.

Out of Blue's view, Bob stopped. "Separate. Get into the countryside. Meet at the campground when you're sure you're not being followed." He gulped some air before continuing, "Good luck."

"You will need more than luck to get across those hay fields with Roland Blue in pursuit," a buxom woman of about forty said. She lifted her vintage brown doeskin skirt and stepped over a loose brick. Short curls of her bobbed brown hair protruded from beneath her olive colored beret.

"Who the hell are you?" asked Will Scathlock

"Curb your tongue, Sport," the woman said, glaring at Will. Turning her attention to Bob, she asked, "You're Bob Brunet, aren't you?"

A circle of smoke floated above her head. In her stubby fingers, she held a pipe with a red clay bowl and a wooden stem.

"Do we know each other?"

"Your picture's been in the newspapers. I keep up with current events from my home in the wilds. You and your two cronies, into my truck." She pointed to the black Model T truck while she spoke. "And shut the door."

Though apprehensive, they obeyed. Bob knew she was right. Flight across country on foot meant sure capture. The three men sardined into the small truck.

"Damn it, Nat, for a little bugger, you take up a gosh awful lot o' space," Will said.

"Don't move. Don't talk," Bob whispered. "Both of you listen."

"Hello, Miss Clorinda," Roland Blue said. He took several deep breaths. "You didn't happen to see three yahoos run past, did you?"

"Couldn't very well miss 'em," Clorinda replied. "They jumped into a sedan that was parked across the tracks. They're long gone."

"Which way?"

"Toward the trunk route."

While Bob watched from behind Clorinda's seat, Roland ripped off his nutria tan hat and flung it to the bricks of the parking lot. "Got away again. Damn 'em," he said. "By the time I find an automobile, they could be in the next county, but I'll round up some deputies and give it a try anyway." He lowered his voice and smiled at Clorinda Vinette. "Can you describe the automobile?"

"Dirty black Model T," Clorinda said.

He shook his head. Then he said, "That's like lookin' for a tree with green leaves. Seems like almost everyone's got a black Ford."

With the false information planted firmly in his brain, Roland Blue picked up his hat, threw back his shoulders, and left.

Clorinda swung aboard her truck and started it. Nobody paid much attention when she drove out of Vinette, but the brief chase caused a stir among the people who had seen it.

CHAPTER NINE
CLORINDA, THE QUEEN OF THE FOREST

"Where to, men?" Clorinda asked.

Bob stuck his head over the top of the leather front seat. He said, "That was close. Thanks. You know my name, but I'm afraid I don't know who you are."

"Miss Clorinda Vinette, Charlemagne Vinette's granddaughter," Nat volunteered. "She's queen of the forest. Pardon my bold tongue, Miss Clorinda. Ah… That's what folks I know call you."

"And, who might you be who knows so much?" Clorinda asked.

"I am Nathaniel Mutch."

"A good choice of names for a peewee like you," Will said. "Not Much. Pretty good, huh, Bob?"

Bob smiled at the pun but said, "Nat's a good fellow and he deserves our respect."

Nathaniel scrambled over Bob, and glowered at Will. "Peewee is it? Let's see if I can't chop you down to my size with my fists."

The truck swayed from side to side while Will and Nat tumbled about, fists flying. Through it all, Nat's peaked cap stuck on his head, but he was no match for sturdy Will Scathlock.

"Get up off my chest, you big ass." He opened his mouth and chomped down on Will's thigh.

"Ouch! You lookin' for some lean meat to build you up?"

"Lean is good, but not stringy," Nat said.

"You're a scrapper, Nat. Here's my hand," Will said. He scrambled off Nat's chest. "Sorry for making fun of you."

"Well, okay." Nat stuck out his hand, but a frown remained on his brow.

"A little fracas now and again keeps us in fighting trim. We'll be ready for the big bout against Quennel and his gang," Bob said.

"You gentlemen are going to have to do more than fight. It's going to take brains to overturn King, Blue, and Quennel," Clorinda said. "Now maybe somebody will answer my question. Where to?"

"The trunk highway to Chicks Oakwood Tavern, then north," Bob said.

"I know the route well. That's the way to my holdings. I have a home and a few acres free and clear," Clorinda said.

"I wish I could say the same," Bob said. "I have a way to go to pay off the mortgage."

Ed Pahnke

"So I read in the newspapers. The King Bank and Quennel are going to foreclose on your mortgage as recompense because of your theft."

"Theft," Bob said. "Damn skunks."

"Can those bast..." Pausing for an alternate word, Will looked at Clorinda, then said, "snakes take your home?"

His face still red from anger, Bob said, "Yes, for now, but eventually we'll get it back. When I win, we all win."

"But how?" Nat asked.

"A good question. Right now, getting money to ransom Richard King is our goal. My goal is to prove I'm innocent of any theft." He stopped and laughed at himself before continuing. "In other words, I don't know yet. I do know we can't sit waiting for things to happen. We've got to make them happen, like organizing resistance, getting my money from the bank, and showing Joe Worman up for the turncoat he is."

"Joe Worman," Clorinda said. "He works for you, foreman or something?"

"Worked," Bob said. "Past tense." Bob told her of his perfidy.

"Maybe I can help," Clorinda said. She wheeled the black truck off the trunk highway onto the one road that cut through the Manitou Hills. Before Bob could say a word, she continued, "When I drive on this road, I figure I'm lucky to have one of Mr. Ford's Model T's. What other automobile could negotiate this nightmare so well? No wonder most folks around here own one."

"I own a Nash, but any help is welcome," Bob said.

Northern Knights

"Stop in for a visit. I'll examine my assets and be ready for you. The lumber business has tumbled to all time lows, but I manage. You'll eat well. I have an Indian cook who can cook. To get to my place, follow this road for three miles after you pass the timber bridge. It's the only bridge you'll see. After you've gone the three miles, you'll reach a narrow lane going north. Stay on it until the lane ends at my home, about a mile and a half. There are no other houses."

"Speaking of trails, there's ours now," Will said. His stomach growled. "It's almost supper time, Bob. I don't want to be gnawing on bones."

Clorinda brought the truck to a halt, and the three men jumped off.

Bob poked his head through the open window on the driver's side. "Would tomorrow be too soon for a visit?"

"About noon will be fine," she said

After Clorinda put the car in gear, it bounced off down the road. Bob gave a perfunctory wave before he turned. Nat and Will had disappeared through the screen of alders onto the path. Bob raced to catch them. Two hours later, they reached the glade.

Hard at work devouring venison and drinking homemade beer, the men belched hardy helloes to the triumphant trio. Bob, Will, and Nat joined in the feasting.

"Any special occasion?" Bob asked.

"Food," a nearby epicure said while wiping beer from his chin with his already damp sleeve.

Will looked at the deer carcass and said, "I knew I'd be gnawing on bones."

Bob thumped Will on the back. "Better gnawing on bones in good company than sitting behind bars. If it wasn't for Clorinda, we could well be in jail right now."

Will was too busy gnawing to comment upon Bob's cheery words.

Taking some venison, Bob walked to the cabin, where he sat on the porch. After a few bites, he stared into the shadows closing in on the glade. He unbuttoned his shirt pocket and felt around inside until he touched the gold wedding band meant for Marian's finger. He didn't look at the ring. The touch of it comforted him, and he withdrew his hand and buttoned the flap on the pocket.

A week had passed since he had escaped arrest at the church, and he wondered how Marian was faring. Did she understand? He had put her out of his mind to concentrate on his new life. He closed his eyes. Now, with time to remember, he saw the two of them together, talking, touching. He had convinced himself it would be wrong for them to see each other until he had proven himself innocent of all charges and reclaimed his property. Yet he must let her know that he was safe and that he kept her in his heart.

Suddenly, a pencil and a scrap of paper were the most important things in his life. Opening his eyes, he looked about the glade. What chance had he of finding such things among the company assembled in the glade, but he had to ask?

Nathaniel sat alone propped against a stump. The smell of wood smoke and charred venison filled the night air.

Bob hunkered next to him and said, "Do you have a pencil and a scrap of paper, Nat?"

Nat looked at Bob, the distant fire reflecting in his eyes. "I'm sure you won't tell the others. They would only poke fun at me. I keep a journal of the day's happenings, and since joining you, the pages have been full. I have pencils in my duffel, and my journal is in my pocket." He patted his vest pocket. "Will a couple of sheets do?"

He flipped the journal open to pages filled with precisely formed words worthy of a penmanship award, and kept turning pages until he found blank ones.

After handing the paper to Bob, Nat dug through his duffel and produced a pencil.

"Thanks, Nathaniel. I'll not say a word about this. I must write to Marian to let her know I'm safe and secure," and under his breath added, "and sentimental."

He returned to his seat on the porch and began writing.

Dear Marian,

When I close my eyes, I see you in your wedding dress standing next to me. I treasure the memory. It sustains me in my fight to prove my innocence and in our search to free Richard King. Oh yes, I have been joined by a group of men in straits as dire as mine.

I dare not let you know my whereabouts. If this letter were to fall into the wrong hands, I would be doomed. I trust you, but who else can I trust? Even Joe Worman is in Quennel's camp.

Ed Pahnke

    I want to be with you, yet I want you safe too. Though we are not separated by great distance, more than a fingertip away is too far.

    Should you be in any sort of danger, please contact Reverend Mike. I meet with him on occasions. Until we are together again, always remember that I love you.

    Bob

    Bob folded the note and put it into his pocket. He'd wait for Cal Little to visit the camp and entrust the message to him.

CHAPTER TEN
MARIAN ALCOTT ENTERS THE FRAY

Marian jumped from her horse, Traveller. The big stallion shook his head. It had been a good ride, and Marian put her arm around Traveller's neck. Refreshed from the canter, even her soul tingled. It seemed to her the only time that she felt happy lately was when she and Traveller were romping across country.

She loosened the horse's saddle girth before she said, "Come along, old boy. Now it's time for a cool off walk." She gently tugged the horse's reins. "You may nuzzle me on the back, if you so desire."

The heavy clump of Traveller's hooves seemed to echo, as though another horse were present, and she turned about to check the farm yard. Closing fast along the lane to the house was a red wagon drawn by a graying chestnut draft horse. Marian knew of the wagon and peddler. Everyone in the county knew of him, but Marian had never met him.

She dropped Traveller's reins to the ground and walked toward the wagon, where it had stopped alongside the stone pump house.

"Morning," the driver said. He whisked the tan cap from his shaggy gray head. "I believe you're Miss Marian Alcott?"

"Yes, I am, but I'm really not interested in any of your merchandise today."

"I'm not here to sell anything, but I wouldn't resist if you was to purchase some of my goods. However, my mission, that's what Bob called it..."

"Bob Brunet?" Marian asked, her eyes brightening, and a smile flickering across her full lips.

"Yes, Miss Marian, none other. I have a message to deliver. Should I wait while you read it? Maybe you'd like to reply?"

"I think that I'd like to read it in private."

"Then I'll be on my way, and catch up with you in a couple of days."

He leaned down and put a neatly folded piece of paper into Marian's hand. She looked about before cramming it into the pocket of her hound's tooth riding jacket.

"Thank you, Mister...?"

"Like the sign says, Miss Marian. I'm Calvin Little. Hup, Thunder."

Horse, wagon, and driver disappeared down the lane. Marian picked up Traveller's reins and walked him about the barnyard. She told herself that Traveller's wellbeing was her immediate concern. Maybe she could stop shaking before reading the note.

When the stallion had cooled down, she removed his tack and hand rubbed him using a linen cloth. Bob's message remained in her pocket. Marian led Traveller into the stable where she groomed him with dandy brush, body brush, and currycomb. Before leading him into his stall, she went over him with a clean towel.

After she had closed the gate to Traveller's stall, Marian took a deep breath.

Only then did she feel brave enough to pull Bob's note out from her pocket. Plunking herself on a wooden bench, she slowly unfolded the piece of paper and immersed herself in the words. She read the letter twice. Each reading bolstered her confidence. She returned the message to her pocket. Finally, she felt she could face her father's reproaches.

"Bob Brunet is a thief," Jeffery Alcott would say. "Gil Quennel likes you. He's rich. Forget Brunet. Soon he won't have even a home, let alone any land. Don't moon around the house. The only one you see, besides me, is that horse."

Looking across the farmyard, Marian saw her father leave their white frame house. His heritage was Down East, and it showed up in his Yankee drawl and in the saltbox house he had built. Nowadays, he seldom smiled, unless he got the better of someone in a deal, but Marian remembered her rawboned father before her mother died. Those had been glorious days. In the ten intervening years, Marian had to prove herself almost daily to her father. It seemed he didn't care for her as a person. He wanted nothing but accomplishments.

Her job as a teacher had pleased him. When Marian fell in love with Bob, Jeffery Alcott didn't congratulate her. Instead, he had wrung his bony hands and complained that she was not the daughter she should have been, but he gave his consent. Gil Quennel was a better man, he had grumbled right up to the wedding day.

Marian patted the pocket where she had put Bob's letter. His words gave her a measure of confidence and dispelled some of her doubts.

"Marian!" Jeffery Alcott called. "Why the devil do you spend so much time with that horse?"

He never pronounced Traveller's name. "That animal" or "that horse" were the extent of his description of Traveller. "Damn" quite often was used in conjunction with his descriptions.

Stepping into the stable, he said, "There you are."

"Yes, Father. I'm going to bathe and change now."

"Good. Gil Quennel is coming for a visit, and you know he likes you. Be polite."

Father and daughter marched back to the house. The house was modern with indoor plumbing and electricity furnished by a water-powered generator in Cauldron Creek. It flowed through the Alcott property.

They entered the house, and Marian noticed a stack of mail on the table next to the door. On top of the stack was a financial statement from "your power company", as they liked to be known, signed as usual by Elliot Bevis.

Father and daughter stood together talking.

"Seeing Gil Quennel reminds me of Bob's plight, but I tolerate him to keep you from nagging me," Marian said.

"A fine attitude. The richest man in the county, who also happens to be eligible, has a yen for you."

"Oh, Father. I'm a person, and I'll marry whom so ever I choose." Not being conceited, she candidly added, "Of course, the man must choose me, too. I don't believe I'm desirable to all men."

Jeffery Alcott glared at his daughter as she minced up the varnished, oak steps. She affected the walk because she wanted to let her father know she was displeased. She went to her room before going to the bathroom. Shortly thereafter, she soaked in a hot tub of water, the water soothing her muscles. She splashed soapsuds on her shoulders and breasts. She dried her hands before spreading Bob's letter on the stand next to the tub. By reading it again, she braced herself for the ordeal. The idea of being polite was impressed on her memory.

On the positive side, she had an opportunity to find out first hand more about the accusations of theft from Gil Quennel. He'd seemed so certain, but he could be wrong. She'd never known Bob to steal, but he'd admitted to having financial problems. Could he have been driven? If she could just talk to him face to face, she'd know. She put her doubts from her thoughts. She'd try to make the best of an unpleasant situation. She began to think about what she'd say.

When she had finished bathing, she dressed. The dress she chose was a pale green print with sloping shoulders and a hemline that reached her mid-calf. Marian's willowy figure suited the style.

When she left her room, she heard voices. Undoubtedly Gil Quennel had arrived. She heard her father laugh, what duplicity. She could count the times on one hand that she had heard her father laugh during the past year.

She flounced down the steps from her room and into the front room. Country Chippendale style furniture, as Marian called them, filled the room, and murals depicting colorful outdoor scenes adorned the walls.

"Gil is here, Marian," her father said. His voice seemed to urge her to hurry.

In a monotone, she said, "How have you been, Gil?"

He rose from the chair on which he had been sitting. When Marian chose to sit on a sofa, Gil scooted over there. Could it be he was leering at her? Certainly that wasn't his natural expression? She turned her attention to her father. Jeffery Alcott smiled contentedly. Did he condone such behavior? It appeared he did.

"Perhaps you have other business, Jeff," Gil said. He winked a beady eye at her father.

"Yes, of course. I'll leave you two young people alone."

Marian winced. Young people indeed. Gil Quennel was every bit of fifteen years older than Marian.

He brushed back his thinning brown hair. "You look lovely today, Marian. Did you put that perfume on especially for me? The odor is enchanting."

"Thank you, Gil." He slid closer to her while they talked. "That's a handsome flannel you're wearing."

"I thought so, too," he replied.

He unbuttoned his double-breasted coat. In attempting to get more comfortable, he touched her knee, and she moved as though she had received a jolt of electricity.

"Do you still feel anything for Brunet?" Gil asked.

"That, is none of your business."

"Of course not. May I hold your hand?"

He put his hand on hers. She moved her hand, and his hand fell on her thigh. He stared at her lips, and she reddened, more from anger than with embarrassment. Who did Gil think he was being so bold?

"You do realize I'm engaged to Bob Brunet, and I'm reluctant to believe your accusations?"

"Him? The life of a hunted fugitive is no life for you, sweet Marian."

"Will you please remove your hand from my thigh?"

A smile crossed his thin lips. In withdrawing his hand, he touched her breast.

"Sorry," he said.

"Not half as sorry as you will be."

She clenched her right hand into a fist and let it fly square into Gil's nose. Blood spurted from it.

"You hit me, you vixen, I'm bleeding." He dabbed at his nose with a white, silk handkerchief. "That was no accident. If you were a man, I'd thrash you. Why did you hit me?"

"If you were half the gentleman you claim to be, you'd know why I hit you."

"Jeff!" Quennel yelled.

Jeffery Alcott ran into the front room.

"My God, Gil. What happened?"

"Before I return, you'd better teach your daughter some manners. I thought you said Marian would welcome my overtures?"

"If there is a next time, ask me instead. Good-by, Mr. Quennel."

"Now wait a second, Marian," her father said. "I say who comes and goes."

"This is my home too." Tears filled her eyes, but she refused to let them flow. "I'm going to my room."

She lifted her hem above her knees and dashed up the stairs. Before she reached the second floor hallway, she knew, somehow, she had to find Bob. Certain that Alice Blue would be the person to ask, Marian determined to seek her out. Bob's note had said Reverend Mike would be the one to contact in the event of peril, and naturally, Alice would be able to influence Reverend Mike. After all, weren't they planning to get married? Marian believed defending her virtue against Gil and her father was reason enough to flee from her own home.

She began throwing sturdy outdoor clothing into a canvas haversack. When it was full to bulging, she took time out to wipe the tears streaking her cheeks. Satisfied that she was composed, she changed to Jodhpurs, Jodhpur boots, and her favorite hounds' tooth jacket. She resented her father's support of Gil Quennel, but he was her father.

She scribbled a note:

Dear Father:

We have different philosophies. I care for a person for what that person is or does, not for what the person possesses. You took the side of Gil Quennel against me when I was in the right. For this reason, and too many more like it, I can no longer stay in our home.

To avoid a quarrel, I am taking this opportunity to leave secretly. My stealth will also serve as a way to leave no clue as to my destination.

Though it may not seem like it to you now, I love you.

Your daughter, Marian

There being no dignified way to sneak away from her home, she recalled a path she had taken in her youth. An ancient hard maple stood outside her bedroom window. Many a stormy night its limbs had scratched mournfully against her windowpane. Amid flashes of lightning and peals of thunder, the raspy scratching had brought shivers of fear into her heart and had driven her deep under her blankets. At other times in her youth, the tree had served as a route to breathing space. Many an early morning, young Marian had descended the tree. Its branches were spaced like a ladder, and she had bounded down them and had been off on Traveller before her father had awakened.

Ed Pahnke

Now her exit would be farewell. She choked back a sob. It wasn't as though she would never see her father again, but maybe it would be never. She looked around her familiar room at the warm possessions that had comforted her. A tattered Raggedy Ann sat on her oak commode. The oak foot post of her canopy bed, worn smooth by her youthful hands, stood straight and sturdy.

Footsteps.

No more time for reminiscence. She pinned the note she had written to her bedspread and slung her haversack over her shoulder. She bounded to the window, lifted the sash, crawled onto the tree, and scampered down to the ground.

As soon as her foot hit the ground, she raced to the stable. Traveller greeted her with a whinny. Marian led him out of his stall, assembled his tack, and readied him for the cross-country ride to Alice Blue's.

CHAPTER ELEVEN
THE SEARCH FOR A HAVEN

Alice Blue and her father lived on the outskirts of Vinette, the county seat of Gamwell County. A black wrought iron fence surrounded the grounds. Even under a bright noontime sun and alongside trees aflame with the season, the two story stone house looked somber. Perhaps it was the gray fieldstone used to construct the timeworn pile that caused the feeling, but people passing the Blue's home often experienced a melancholy pang, or so they claimed.

After tying her horse to the fence, Marian marched to the heavy, wooden front door. No feeling of melancholy affected her. Her thoughts were fixed on seeing Bob. When she reached the entrance, she whacked the black knocker against the door.

Moments later, Alice swung the door open.

"My goodness, Marian, and you brought your horse too. Come inside."

A saucy smile lit her face. She grabbed Marian's hand and dragged her inside.

"I don't want you to get away." Her pink Marcella broadcloth frock rustled while she led Marian into the front room. "I have heard absolutely nothing from you since that terrible day at the Church at the Corners. I respected your wish for seclusion, but I'm happy you've come to visit. Sit on the divan. I'll pop into the kitchen and get some tea. Or maybe you prefer coffee?"

"I'd prefer to tell you the reason for my call."

The bright smile on Alice's face instantly faded, to be replaced by a shocked look.

"Well, Marian, I see that you've not gotten over your snit about being left at the altar."

"I have a new snit now. Better yet, I have a pair of snits." In her mind, she resolved to be careful of her pronunciation of snit. "If you don't help me, I'll have three snits."

"I'm all ears."

"I won't make a smart comment about your ears," Marian said.

She laughed and rose from the blue-gray divan. The two friends embraced. Marian quickly told Alice about Bob's letter, Gil Quennel's rakish behavior, and her father's consent to Gil's actions.

Then Marian said, "Before your father returns from work, please contact your Reverend Mike and ask him to take me to Bob's hideout. I feel like a gun moll in a pulp magazine, and I don't like the feeling. I must know for certain that Bob is what he claims he is, a wrongly accused man. I want to believe in him. I can't love him otherwise, but I don't understand why Father is so certain Bob's guilty?

"Why would Gil lie about a theft, certainly not just to have the freedom to pursue me?

"I must see and talk with Bob. Otherwise I'll return to teaching, and I won't be so easily coaxed away next time if my love's been exploited.

"You're my best friend, and I trust you. I also have faith in Reverend Mike, but he too may be wrong about Bob. I must learn the truth for myself."

"I'll help you, Marian. Of course I don't know Bob's whereabouts. I don't think Mike knows either, but I'll convince him we should help you." She patted Marian's hand. "Meantime, we have to find a place for you to stay, and I'm sure my father won't allow you to stay here once he knows why you left home."

She paused and frowned, as if thinking. "The Church at the Corners has some rooms in the loft, as you know. I'll drive you there after I talk with Mike. Perhaps he'll keep Traveller in the pasture behind his house because I have a feeling Bob won't be able to board a horse in his lair."

After Alice phoned Mike Rood, she and Marian jumped into Roland Blue's 1930 Model A Ford Roadster. Judging from the way Alice drove the maroon automobile, she had decided she would make the trip so harrowing that Marian would consider any future experience tame by comparison. She drove directly to the Church at the Corners.

It was Wednesday, and the church was empty.

Upon entering the church, the two young women trudged up the stairs to the loft. Although they had been friends for years, Marian had never known that Alice could drive. At Marian's request, they settled into a room other than the one they had occupied before the wedding.

Marian looked about the small, gray room at a marred wooden table and two sagging, leather easy chairs, a far cry from her own comfortable room. For a moment, she thought about going back home, demeaning herself before her father. "No," she said aloud and drove the easy way from her mind.

Marian faced the usually vivacious Alice, but she remained silent. Why? She was usually such a chatterbox. "I've burdened you with my problems, but tell me about you. How are you and Reverend Mike getting along? Is there any thawing in your father's opinion about him?"

"About the same," Alice said.

"That bad? Do you care to talk about your problem?"

When Alice began talking, there was no doubt that she did want to talk about her problem.

"I love a wonderful man, but Father considers ministry to be a sissy occupation."

"But Reverend Mike was a lumberjack before he became a minister," Marian said. "Doesn't that count for anything?"

"Not according to my father. He says that a man who follows Mike's profession is less than a man. I explain till I'm blue on the face, if you'll pardon the expression, that Mike had a calling from God."

"My explanations do no good, and Father won't talk about the matter any more. I'm exasperated. Part of me says elope, but Mike thinks Father will come around. He wants family harmony, if possible."

"So it's a stalemate?" Marian said. She shook her head. "Do you think your father is right about Bob?" She grabbed Alice's hands hoping to be comforted by her answer.

"The more I'm home since college, the less I respect Father's occupation, and it's not being sheriff that bothers me. It's some of the things he does or condones that appear less than honest to me. I don't share my opinions with Father, but I tell Mike. Mike believes that your Bob is innocent, but I'm not sure what to believe. I don't feel completely right about reporting Father's business to Mike, but I think I'm doing the right thing, most of the time.

"Did I answer your question, Marian?"

The two women sank back into their chairs, and they became silent while awaiting Mike Rood. His home was in Langston because there were no living quarters at the church. From Langston to Alice's home, to the pasture, and to the church could take a couple of hours.

Two hours passed.

The thump of clodhoppers on wooden steps broke the silence. "That has to be my Mike. He has the heaviest tread of anyone I've ever met. A misstep by him when we're dancing, and I could have flat feet on the tops."

Alice scooted to the doorway and looked down the hall. "Mike, over here."

Ed Pahnke

Reverend Michael Rood smiled broadly. "Hi, Hon," he said. He shifted the western style saddle that he had balanced on his shoulder. "I rode Traveller to the pasture like you asked. I walked from there since my automobile is in front of your house. I figured this would be a safe place to stow the saddle and blanket. Hi, Marian."

Marian shot out of the room and ran to Mike.

"How good to see you, Reverend Mike," she said before giving him a peck on his cheek. Mike blushed to the color of the red saddle blanket.

"Honestly, Marian, you'll try almost anything to get Mike to guide you to Bob's camp." Alice laughed lightly.

Marian turned to Alice and said, "As if I have never given Reverend Mike a kiss before, but you needn't be jealous when Reverend Mike and I are alone on the trail. I promise not to vamp him."

Mike listened wide-eyed to the conversation.

"I have eyes only for Bob." Again Marian turned to Mike. "You will take me to Bob's hideout - how I hate that word – won't you?"

Marian had no trace of a smile on her lips. Flirting was not in her nature, friendship and honesty were. She didn't wait for an answer. "Follow us into the room. I know that saddle is heavy."

Marian took Alice's arm and hustled her through the doorway into the room.

Once inside, Mike dropped the saddle and blanket in the empty closet. Turning, he said, "I understand your need to see Bob. At least, I think I do, but…"

"But?" Marian said.

"I don't know the way. I have to wait for Bob's agent to contact me."

"Bob has an agent? How sinister," Alice said. "Is this Gamwell County or some Eastern principality? If Bob is captured, he may well be thrown into a black hole and have the key thrown away. Oh, I had a terrible thought. My father will be the jailer. I'll have to give him a Mickey Finn, get the keys, and break Bob out. In his emaciated state, I'll probably have to carry him."

Mike knew from experience to let Alice run out of steam. So did Marian, but she was impatient.

"May we turn this melodrama off, Alice? Reverend Mike has more important things to do. For instance, how long do you expect it will take before you see this agent?"

Already convinced of the necessity of Marian's undertaking, Mike said, "I should be back here with the information tomorrow morning. Maybe the agent will guide you. Bob says the less I know about his activity, the better.

"As for your stay, there's a pump in the kitchen, downstairs, and I'll put some food there for you while you're here."

Probably remembering their greeting and the furor, Mike held out his hand to Marian. She gripped it with both hands and said, "Thank you, Mike, I mean Reverend Mike."

"Mike is fine. Good-bye till tomorrow."

A tear in her eye, Marian gave Alice an embrace and said, "Careful now."

"I'll drive you to my house to get your car, Mike," Alice said.

"I didn't know you could drive, Hon."

"I learned today," Alice replied.

Hand in hand, Mike and Alice left the Church at the Corners.

Marian sank into the brown, leather chair, her mind in a whirl. Would her father learn of her whereabouts, storm to the church, and cause a scene? How long would she have to wait for the agent? Who was he, and would he consent to guide her?

CHAPTER TWELVE
WOODLAND DISCOVERIES

Bob and Will had been tramping through the forest for over two hours. They had yet to see a house worthy of the name. Twice they saw open sided log lean-tos nestled close to live springs. The ashes in front of the shelters were cold. No people saluted them with vigorous waves, but fugitives don't crave strangers' company, attention or questions.

Rather than chance being seen on the one artery through the Manitous, Bob and Will hiked west across country, north of the bridge Clorinda had mentioned as a landmark.

While they tramped along the bank of a nameless stream, Bob saw two sleek, brown otters frolicking in the water.

"Look at them, Will," Bob whispered.

"I never seen no animal that has more fun than otters," Will said in a low voice. "Wish we could enjoy life like them."

Bob thumped Will on his back. "Let's push on, old friend."

About an hour later, they came to a crossroad.

"That must be the road leading to Miss Clorinda's home."

"Hell," Will said, "I seen deer paths wider than that. How can she get that truck through?"

Weeds grew in the center between two ruts. Weary, both men slogged along the lane. They expected to see a house around each bend or at the crest of each hill, but they continued to see only tree filled vista.

Bob's smile slowly vanished, and Will continued to grumble heartily. "I don't believe there is a house at the end of this road. "We'll keep goin' till we get swallowed up by the forest and get putrefied."

Bob wondered if Will meant petrified and was about to ask when he saw a file of moss covered stones stretching along the road. "What's that?" He answered his own question. "A stone wall, and I bet it surrounds Clorinda Vinette's house."

"If it's anything like other distances around here, we'd have a shorter walk followin' the Great Wall of China."

"Where did you hear about the Great Wall of China?"

"I seen pictures, Bob. I ain't so dumb as you look."

If someone else had made such a statement, Bob might have taken offense. As it was, he smiled and found the energy to quicken his pace. Reluctantly, Will did, too. After less than a quarter of a mile, Bob sighted a set of wooden gateposts. The space between trees increased indicating the area had been brushed out. Straining their eyes, they saw a house set on a rise overlooking a meadow. Beyond it was a small lake.

"What time is it, Bob?"

Bob looked at his pocket watch. Before his father died, he had given the pewter-backed timepiece to Bob. He rubbed the watch on his shirt before opening the cover. He said, "Almost noon."

Will looked up at the sun. "That's about right. I'm checking to see if your watch is accurate. Do you think we can make it for dinner?"

"I seem to recall you claiming Indian cooks were one step up from the Borgias," Bob said.

"What's that?"

"A family of poisoners."

"Hell no. Some Injuns has a knack for fixin' damn good chow, not as good as you cook, though. My mouth waters at the thought of Injun food."

Bob knew Will's mouth watered at the thought of any food.

"Keep walking. Let's save the talking for around the dinner table." Will took his own advice and double-timed.

The road crossed a field and skirted a clump of birches at the front door. The roof of the two-story house was covered with hand-rived shakes, and a stone chimney protruded through the center of the roof. A wisp of smoke floating from the chimney told them somebody was home. A set of casement windows gleamed on each side of the heavy oak door.

They followed the road, and, a few minutes later, they walked up the wooden steps. Bob reached for the brass doorknocker and gave the door a thump. Before the echo died away, the door swung open. Clorinda stood in front of them dressed much the same as she had been when they first met. The red bowl of her pipe stuck out from her doeskin jacket. She carried a copy of the Vinette Weekly Journal.

"Come on in, fellows. Did you enjoy your hike to my corner of the hills?"

Without answering, Bob looked around the entrance hall. The lodge was constructed of white pine logs, probably split. Inside, the plastered walls were decorated with murals showing scenes from mythology. Satyrs romped with woodland nymphs in one. The King of Wood guarded the tree with the golden bough in the other.

"Corner is right," Will said. "We must be 'bout at the west end of the Manitous, and my feet feel like they trod on every bump in the hills."

"That may be, but there are a few more miles before the terrain begins to level out around Homestead Lake. Follow me. We can sit and talk in the front room."

They sat on a maroon velvet sofa that faced a set of casement window. Two large cases containing a collection of guns stood against a far wall.

Will had been staring at the newspaper that Clorinda continued to hold in her hand. He asked, "Anything about us in the newspaper?"

She held up the newspaper. "This? I picked it up before I met you two boys yesterday. No, but there's a story about John King from the bank. He and Gil Quennel have mounted a drive to raise money to pay Richard's ransom. They gave a list of major contributors to the newspaper. Have you boys ever heard of Elliot Bevis of the District Power Company? He donated fifty dollars to head the list."

"I remember a Revis Potter, but no Elliot Bebvis," Will said.

"Bevis," she corrected him.

"My name's not down there anywhere, is it?" A rare smile flitted across his lips. He seemed not to pay any attention to her interruption. "You're about as likely to find my name on that list as you are to find any of that money going to Richard's kidnappers."

While Will and Clorinda talked, Bob's gaze fastened on the red pipe bowl that protruded from her pocket.

"I don't remember ever having seen a pipe like the one sticking out of your pocket. Where did you get it?"

Clorinda removed the pipe from her pocket and held it up.

Bob looked even closer. Why had this handsome woman decided to smoke a pipe? Never having seen a pipe between her lips, Bob couldn't imagine the effect it had on her attractiveness.

"There's an Indian who works for me. He cuts the bowls out at the Indian Pipestone quarry on the far-western fringe of the hills."

"These hills? I never heard of no such a quarry," Will said.

"It's not nearly as famous as the one in Minnesota, but it's served the tribes here about for ages."

"How does the pipe taste?" Bob asked. "I have a peddler friend who might be able to sell them."

"I enjoy smoking the pipe, but I don't think Leo Long Mane would want to chance other folks finding the quarry and mining it. What he does, he does for Indians."

"Leo Long Mane?" Bob said. "Does he work for you?" He slid forward on the sofa to hear Clorinda's answer.

"Leo's a good worker. Oh, sometimes I catch him looking at a wild flower or up at a raven in a pine. Moments later, he'll be hard at work again. He'll be mending fence again soon for me. I suppose chipping out red pipe bowls comes ahead of lifting stones into place on my fence."

"What tribe does he come from?" Bob asked. Without waiting for an answer, he continued, "Chippewa? Menominee? What?"

"I really don't know." She wrinkled her brow as though trying to think while she spoke. "He drifted down from the Apostles a couple of years ago. Fished and hunted there, he said, and worked for a rich bugger on Hermit Island. The Bad River Reservation is close to the Apostles. I suppose he could've come from there.

"Mostly, he is a lone wolf. He tramps all over with those pipe bowls. He claims he's preserving the ways of his forefathers. He calls himself *Anishinabe*. When I ask what that means, he says it means first man."

"*Anishinabe* is what the Chippewa call themselves," Bob said, smiling. "I'd like to meet him. Does he live close by?"

"Some folks think that wild devil kidnapped Richard King," Will said. "Me and Bob seen an unsigned ransom note. Didn't we, Bob?"

Bob nodded.

"We was helping Mike Rood at the Church at the Corners when the note got slipped under the door," Will said. "A couple o' minutes later, John King showed up at the door and said he got a telephone call tellin' him to be there. He also claimed he saw an Indian who he identified as Leo Long Mane hanging around the Church at the Corners that night. Mike give the note to John King, like he was directed on the envelope. Me and Bob hung over John King's shoulder when he read the note. It was all in the newspaper."

"I don't always see all the local newspaper. I go into town once a week and sometimes have to settle for a down state newspaper.

"And nobody mentioned anything to you about Leo Long Mane being sought for questioning?" Bob said.

"This is the first I've heard about it. Leo works hard, when he works for me, and I can't believe he could be involved. What makes it more difficult to believe is that Leo can't write. Oh, he can sign his name, but that's about all."

"Will he be at the Pipestone quarry today? I'd like to ask him a few questions," Bob said.

"I don't know if I should tell you since he's more a friend than an employee."

"We can't afford to get involved with the law. We have to talk, that's all. Neither Will or I carry a gun unless we're out hunting or expecting trouble," Bob said. "We carry only sheath knives."

"Well, I suppose." She hesitated before she said, "The last time I saw him, the day before yesterday it was, he said he was going to the pipestone quarry today, and then who knows."

"What's he look like?" Will asked.

"He's all bone and sinew, and two or three inches taller than me, I'd say. I'm five foot five inches in my stockings. If he weighs a hundred and ten, that's tops, but he's a holy terror if he gets riled."

"We're going there to talk, not fight," Bob said.

Bob had no intention of letting Leo Long Mane escape before having a conversation with him, and he'd do anything to gain this end. Then a smile settled on his lips. He wanted to assure Clorinda his attentions were peaceful. Also, he figured he might be close to finding Richard King.

Bob sat back on the couch, adjusted his cap, and rubbed the back of his neck. He said, "Well..."

"You boys aren't leaving right away, are you? I thought you two would have dinner with me. We can discuss money over the meal."

"We can't disappoint her, can we, Bob?"

"Dinner sounds too good to pass up," Bob said.

They rose from the sofa and trooped behind Clorinda into the dining room. Three places had been set on the table that looked large enough to seat twelve. It and the chairs that surrounded it were mahogany with spiraled legs.

Meeting Clorinda in town had been fortunate. They'd been saved from capture, alerted to the whereabouts of a possible kidnapper, and were about to be served dinner on China with linen napkins and a white tablecloth.

Bob shoved his right hand into his shirt pocket, squeezed the gold wedding band between his fingers, and thought of Marian. Sitting along side her would have made the setting complete.

Will stifled a belch. Clorinda puffed her pipe. When Bob finally saw her puffing on a pipe, it seemed natural. He shifted about on his chair. "Thanks for a fine dinner, Miss Clorinda. We welcome you to our side and thanks again for offering to contribute a few dollars now and again. But, most of all, I'm grateful for your confidence in my innocence."

Clorinda blushed and smiled. "My pleasure."

Northern Knights

Bob stood. "We have to be on our way." He walked to the stone fireplace. Embers glowed inside, and a collection of knickknacks decorated the pine mantel. "Can you give us directions to the pipestone quarry?"

After blowing a cloud of smoke into the air, Clorinda said, "From here you have to strike out across country. There are no trails going west and darn few going north and south. You can see Charlemagne Lake out the window. If you stay along the south shore, you'll reach a path starting at the lake. Continue west another couple of miles until you reach a blazed trail. Go south on it about a half a mile. You'll run into the diggings.

"Leo is a good fellow, and I don't think he's a kidnapper, but I hope he can help you."

While saying good-by, Bob was both eager to leave and anxious about leaving. He wondered if they should first return to their camp for guns. He certainly didn't want to ask Clorinda for weapons. That request would loose her as a friend and ally, but if Leo Long Mane were a kidnapper, he was likely to be armed. Bob's and Will's knives would be no match for him. On the other hand, going back to camp would delay them until the next day. Would Leo Long Mane stay at the quarry another day?

Tomorrow could be too late. If they were going to find him, it would have to be that same day. Surprise was the only element they had on their side, and they had to use it to their advantage, or they could fine themselves dead.

CHAPTER THIRTEEN
LEO LONG MANE AND THE INDIAN PIPESTONE QUARRY

Their feet thumping on the hard packed trail, Bob and Will skirted Charlemagne Lake. Cattails choked the shoreline. Farther out in the water, pickerelweed invaded the lake. The swirl of a large fish made Bob want to stop and try his luck, but stopping to fish had become only a dream.

Brown ferns spilled onto the trail. High in the birches and hemlocks, wind was the song of the great forest. Not everyone listened to the song, but both Bob and Will did. The sound drew them outdoors and lightened their hearts.

When past the lake, Bob saw ruffed grouse pecking away on the forest floor. Bob smiled. Hiawatha's chickens. When approached, they took grudgingly to the air.

There had already been two frosts that season, and many leaves from the popples lay on the forest floor. Bob and Will plowed through them.

Northern Knights

Those yellow leaves remaining on the branches waved down at them from beneath deep blue sky. For a while, the route followed a stream through a valley. Lack of rain left only a trickle of water in the bed. Veering from the stream, they had to scramble up and down rugged hills.

Bob hoped Leo Long Mane had kidnapped Richard King. Though the word of John King was not proof, Bob wanted Leo to be guilty. He convinced himself that Indians had odd moral values and were lazy besides. Leo Long Mane was not a member of the community, and he wouldn't be missed. That was the good part. If he had harmed Richard... He put that thought out of his mind. Richard had to be alive to force John from the bank and solve the problems of the county. Bob itched for a fight.

He stopped. What was he thinking about wanting a man to be guilty because he was different?

The few Indians he had known worked hard when given a chance. Clorinda had said Leo Long Mane worked hard for her. They were friendly, a bit clannish perhaps, but they had to be. White men had kept them at arms length. They knew their country. If alcohol did not take their souls, they were good family men. In many cases, white men had sent red men off on the wrong trail, and maybe Bob was too.

"Why'd you stop, Bob?"

Bob started walking. He said nothing, but decided to consider Leo Long Mane as a person, not as an Indian.

When they found the blazed trail Clorinda had described, Will said, "I was beginning to think we missed this path."

"I don't know exactly how far we have to travel before we reach the quarry. Maybe this Long Mane fellow will spook if he hears us. I say we stop talking starting right now."

"Oh, sure. You say that because you want the last word. Okay, you're the boss."

Will clamped his jaw shut and pulled his leather cap down over his ears. They walked on in silence. While they walked, the path grew wider and sloped downward toward a shallow canyon.

A short time later. Bob and Will entered an area cluttered with pink rocks. On either side of them, thick layers of pink or gray quartzite and thin bands of grayish-red and blood red pipestone made up the steep walls. Bob felt awe at the place, the way one would be by a great cathedral.

They advanced using boulders and spindly popples for cover. When they peeked from behind a crumbling boulder, they saw a fire. Nearby, an Indian sat smoking. Though his back was turned to them, he fit the description Clorinda had given. His black shoulder length hair rubbed his wool coat collar whenever he turned his head from side to side, as if to hear what he couldn't see.

The Indian seemed oblivious of their presence. The only cover close to him was a pile of freshly cut logs. It lay to his left, and Bob pointed at the logs. Remaining crouched, they made their way toward the logs. The wind stirring in the treetops masked the sound of their approach, and, added to that, their footsteps landed as lightly as autumn leaves falling on the forest floor. When they reached the logs and could not see the Indian, Bob motioned Will to circle to one side of the logs while he went the other way.

Upon reaching the end of the pile, Bob peered around the corner. A green twig from a protruding log scrapped his nose. He scratched it, and blinked his eyes in wonder.

Where the Indian had been sitting seconds before, only a campfire remained. The firewood continued to glow under a coat of white ash. Bob looked back for Will, but he had disappeared, probably around the other side of the stack. Not knowing where the Indian would next appear, Bob moved forward cautiously.

When he reached the front corner of the stack, he expected to see Will. He didn't, but he heard a thud and a string of epithets. Abandoning caution, Bob dashed to the other end of the logs.

He found Will prone on the ground. The slim Indian sat on Will's back. He didn't struggle because the Indian held a hunting knife against his throat.

"Why do you sneak up on people?" the Indian asked. "What do you want here?"

Intent on questioning Will, the Indian didn't seem to hear Bob's noisy approach. Bob's feet grated on the rocky surface before he launched himself and dove at the Indian. He intended to knock him off Will, but at the place he expected to slam his shoulder into him, he met no resistance. A moment later, his flight stopped abruptly when he thudded into the butt end of a log with his shoulder. Stunned, he tumbled onto his back.

Shoulder throbbing, he looked for the Indian. He didn't have long to wait. The Indian, his face expressionless, lunged at him. Bob aimed a kick at the Indian's dead pan. The blow struck true. His head popped back, and

Ed Pahnke

his hunting knife sailed through the air. Dazed, he regained his feet, reeling about.

Bob scrambled to his feet, and swung a roundhouse that landed on the red man's cheek. The Indian crumpled like soggy newspaper.

Will gained his feet, and helped Bob pin the Indian's shoulders to the earth.

"What do you guys want?" the Indian asked. "Why did you sneak up on a fellow?" A quizzical, innocent look held on his pockmarked face.

"We've come to talk, not fight," Bob said.

"I'm as ready to talk as the next guy. Starting with a fight is a hell of a way to begin. Sneaking up on a *Anishinabe* don't show good sense neither. We can smell you guys, especially down wind. You two walk real soft. I thought there was one man with a big mixture of smells."

Bob tightened his grip on the Indian.

"Wouldn't it have been better to walk up to me and said hello? We would have been on friendly terms straight off. I don't trust a man who takes my freedom. I've decided to let my spirit loose. You'll be able to hurt only my body."

"We don't want to harm you, but we have some questions," Bob said. "Are you Leo Long Mane?"

"Yes. I don't have no money. It's been years since I seen a dollar bill. Are they still green? All I ever see is small change. I sell pipes for pennies."

"What have you done with Richard King? Who's in this kidnapping with you?" Bob said.

"And they call me crazy. I ain't done nothin' wrong. I ain't never seen Richard King."

"We have a witness that says different," Will said.

"That's right," Bob said. "He claims you were loitering around the Church at the Corners on the evening the first ransom note was found."

"I don't know nothing about no damn ransom note. I was at the Church at the Corners only once. I delivered a note that Joe Worman gave to me. Ask him. He said to drop it off and leave."

"How do you know Joe?" Bob asked.

"Mister Worman hired me and a couple of my friends to clear out brush around his boss's mill. I think his boss's name is Bob Brunet."

"I remember that, Bob," Will said. "Joe said the work needed to be done, but that wasn't Joe's writing on the note. I'd recognize his. Whoever wrote that note must've got a Palmer Method certificate when he was a kid. Joe scribbles, like me."

"Go on, Leo," Bob said nodding to Will.

"Later, Mr. Worman gave me a dime to deliver the note."

"We got to talk with Joe," Will said.

Quiet under their grips, Leo asked, "Are one of you guys Bob Brunet?"

Not yet convinced, Bob said, "I am, but I told you that I ask the questions. How does it happen you knew nothing about Richard King's kidnapping and you were suspected of the kidnapping?"

"I've been back in the bush. I get plenty of work and food from Miss Clorinda, damn little money though."

"I think he's telling it straight, Bob. Looks like he's an outlaw like us, but the sheriff will believe Joe Worman's word over his. We've got to face Joe and get him to tell the truth."

"Convince him by whatever means needed," Bob said, "but where the hell do we find him? I warned him to leave the county, and his dust is probably only a memory. We can figure Gil Quennel is at the bottom of this. Joe's his man, I think, but I can't figure Quennel for a kidnapper. We're enemies all right. He's greedy, and he bends the law, but I never heard of him breaking it. Damn, I don't know."

"This is one hell of a mystery. I'm stumped for sure," Will said.

"Let me join up with you, Bob. Maybe together we can clear both our names," Leo said.

"Should we let this skinny bugger throw in with us, Bob?" Will eyed Leo.

Bob and Will stood. Leo looked as though he was pasted to the ground.

"Give us your hands, Leo," Bob said.

He gripped their hands, and they yanked him to his feet.

"There's no doubt that we need good men, and we also need eyes throughout the county. Stay away from towns and sheriffs. You continue as usual, but you should know how to contact us. Tell Miss Clorinda when you want to talk to us. We'll contact her from time to time to set up meetings."

"You know Miss Clorinda?"

"She told us where to find you," Bob said, "and she also told us that you were no kidnapper. Now we know for sure she was right."

Northern Knights

After they had shaken Leo's hand, Bob and Will began the long trek home. They had made a new friend, but they were no closer to Richard King's kidnapper or to clearing Bob's name than they had been before. Maybe Will was right. They had about as much chance of finding Richard King as finding a raindrop in a river, but they had to keep trying.

CHAPTER FOURTEEN
THE REUNION

"There they are, at last. Bob and Will!"

Shouts greeted Bob's return to the hidden forest glade. At first Bob thought the worst, that an accident had happened, the hideout had been discovered. He steeled himself for a fight or a foot race.

Smiles would be absent if there were trouble. But welcoming grins radiated from each weathered face. Certainly his return after a few hours absence didn't deserve such an outpouring.

He continued to wonder until he saw his cabin. He rubbed his eyes and looked again. A woman stood framed in the doorway.

"Marian," he said almost to himself. "Am I dreaming?"

When she moved toward him, she seemed to glide across the meadow. She wore one of the forest-green Filson cruisers that Cal had bought with some of the money Bob withdrew from his bank account. If it hadn't been for her slim, feminine figure, she could have passed for one of the men.

"Bob!"

Northern Knights

She floated into his arms. They kissed and embraced to a chorus of cheers and a round of applause. Both reddened. Bob acknowledged the crowd's cheer with a wave while Marian pulled him toward the log cabin. Bob grasped her hand. Though pleased to see Marian, he also planned his approach to the delicate subject of her departure. Delicate indeed, he had to ask her to leave, for her safety, but how would he begin?

Cal stood in front of the building waiting for them. "I guided Miss Marian here. Reverend Mike asked me to because she was being harassed by Gil Quennel..."

"I'll explain my reason for being here to Bob when we're alone," Marian said.

"Yes, Miss Marian," Calvin Little said. "Before I go, Bob, I have a message for you from Reverend Mike."

"Go ahead."

"Dick Legh, the mayor of Vinette, wants to talk with you this Sunday, if that's possible. He needs your help. Get word to me, and I'll tell Reverend Mike."

"My help? I don't know what I can do, but I'll meet with him. Where?"

"About three at the Church at the Corners. Reverend Mike says there's nothing quieter than the church on a Sunday afternoon. If he thinks his church is quiet on a Sunday," Cal said, "he should see my wagon, talk about quiet. What should I tell him?"

"Tell Mike I'll be there. You'd better get back to business. Thanks."

He shook Cal's hand, and the big man strode away.

Bob faced Marian. With one arm, he gave her a squeeze around her waist. With his free hand, he touched the gold wedding band in his shirt pocket. When they entered the cabin, he buttoned the pocket containing the ring.

They didn't speak but looked into each other's eyes. Marian snuggled to his chest. Bob knew he had to begin talking, or he'd weaken.

"Marian, it's wonderful to see you, to hold you, but my letter — your safety?"

She explained about her clash with Quennel and her father. In her mind there were no alternatives. "Bob, I don't know how to phrase this. But, Father seems so certain that you're guilty, and Gil Quennel wouldn't fabricate such a lie with the sole motive of getting rid of a rival for my affection. They believe you're a thief, but I'm not certain. Please say you're innocent."

Bob listened intently. When she began to voice her doubts, he felt himself getting angry, but he told himself that he'd have doubts too. No matter how much a person loves another, assurance may be needed. He studied her lips before looking into her eyes. "I am innocent. For some reason, Quennel wants all the real estate he can get, including my property. I think that's his real motive, and with me out of the way, he'll add my land to what he already owns."

Wanting to believe him, Marian paced back and forth digesting his words. What he said made sense. She threw her arm over Bob's shoulders. "You convinced me. You do know I've come to stay."

"I love you too much to let you stay here."

They had seated themselves at the pine-topped table holding hands, but she wrenched her hand free and said, "You won't let me stay?" Her face was flushed. "What safer place is there than with you?"

She stood, tears clouding her eyes. She turned toward the side window. Bob saw her reflection in the glass. He wanted to hold her and beg her to stay.

"Sweetheart, I want you beside me, but not while I'm a fugitive. This isn't a family camp. Some of the men have wives and children, but they travel to their families to take them whatever food and funds we can provide."

Marian crossed her arms in front of her and continued to face away from Bob.

"There's the danger that Sheriff Blue will search us out and raid us. We might have to fight to save ourselves. Then it's run again. I want you safe, but if you're seen with me, you'll be treated like a fugitive, too."

He put his hands on her shoulders. She whirled to face him and pushed away his hands. "Don't treat me like a china doll. I'm a countrywoman. I can ride and shoot, but if I'm not needed now; perhaps I should leave, for good. Maybe you don't want to be tied down or married to me. Your trouble is a convenient escape from me, and you're using it. This camp is remote enough so that nobody could ever find it."

"I have no doubts about our love and marriage," Bob said, thinking to himself that Marian might be right, "I'm telling you the truth when I say there's a likelihood that somebody from Quennel's side could find us. If one of my men is followed, he may well lead the law here."

"Perhaps you want me to return to Gil Quennel. I'm certain he'll be happy to have me back so he can try to seduce me again."

"I'll deal with him in short order."

"Ha! You're afraid to stick your head out of your hole in this forest."

Marian's words hurt Bob. Did she think him a coward? "I promised to clear my name and reclaim my property. Those aren't the vows of a coward."

She looked down at the floor. "I know you're not a coward," she whispered. "I'm sorry. The words were meant to hurt you. I thought being together might help you."

"I don't want to send you back to your home. There's danger there too. I also know you're as good an archer as there is in this county. You could supply game without the noise of gunfire, but aside from the danger, being here together would rouse our desires."

"I am glad you're attracted to me. To all intents and purposes we're already married. It's right for us to have physical longings, but my desires are in check. Men think lovemaking is all-important. Perhaps your libido can be satisfied by another woman?"

"I promised you that I'd be true to you, and I am. What I'm saying is, we shouldn't be in a common law situation. Your nearness and the danger of capture will have me listening for footsteps behind me rather than looking forward to solutions."

He frowned for a moment and then smiled. "I have it. There's a safe haven for you in the Manitou Hills. Clorinda Vinette helped Will, Nat, and me escape from Roland Blue."

While Bob spoke Marian's expression brightened.

"I'll be able to visit you in her house in the forest, and you'll be safe from that skunk, Quennel."

"Oh, Bob, that sounds wonderful, but may I stay here with you, for the night?"

"You shall have this cabin to yourself overnight."

"I'll tell Will and Nat where we're going tomorrow."

After Bob left her alone in the cabin, Marian relived each kiss, each caress, and each word. While preparing for bed, she listened to the fire crackle in the fireplace and wondered where she would be in twenty-four hours. What sort of person was the reclusive Clorinda Vinette? Did she really live like a queen in a castle deep in the forest with Indian workers?

Marian hoped she'd be comfortable in bed wearing only a brassiere and panties. Her one nightgown was packed away. After she shed her blouse and baggy trousers, she looked at her fair skin in the fire's glow. Before diving under the covers, she sunk the metal dipper deep into a pail of icy water. Her mouth felt numbed by the cold. Resting her head on her hand, she remembered her classes of school children. Her eyelids grew heavy, and her head slipped off her hand and sunk into the pillow. She fell asleep.

The day dawned bright, sunny. It continued that way all the time Bob and Marian tramped the forest paths.

"I hope we're not going to impose upon Miss Vinette."

"Don't worry about that, Sweetheart. Miss Clôrinda is a gracious person."

Marian had been waiting for a kiss and an embrace throughout the course of the trek. When Bob said they were about a mile from Clorinda's home, she knew the forest fastness would soon be coming to an end.

"Bob, stop," she said. "Why have you been so distant this morning? I need your arms about me, your lips on mine. I have to be reassured before you leave."

"I've wanted to embrace you from the first step, but I shoved the thoughts from my mind. The…"

"Shut up," Marian said. "Do it."

Bob stopped in his tracks and stared at her. "Marian!"

Even she could not believe she'd been so bold, but she didn't stop with words. She clamped her arms around him and kissed his mouth, his neck. After pushing his cap off his head, she tousled his hair.

He dropped her haversack on the path.

"I need your kisses," she whispered in his ear.

They remained in each other's arms. "I do love you, Bob. I've missed being with you. I admit I had my doubts about you, and I prayed to God that I might trust you without doubting your innocence, but it took your words to convince me. Do you think less of me?"

"I understand. Rather than thinking of us as being torn apart, think of our time together as strengthening our bond. Remember I miss you, and I'll visit often."

After kissing again, they each took a step back. Bob still held Marian's hand in a firm grip.

"Add my name to those helping you to bring justice back to Gamwell County," Marian said.

Bob released her hand and stooped to retrieve her haversack from the trail. Laughing, Marian nudged him with her hip. He sprawled over a wild strawberry patch. Reaching out, he tried to grab her leg and drag her down too, but she evaded his grasp.

"You, rascal," he said, smiling and scrambled to his feet.

With Marian in the lead, they raced along the trail toward Clorinda Vinette's lodge. Both laughed and puffed, breathless, when Bob finally caught her.

He hugged her and lifted her off her feet. "If you learn anything about what's happening in our county, contact us. We can add ever bit of information to what we know. That way, even being apart, we'll be working together." Nearby, they found a rivulet where they washed and refreshed themselves before walking hand in hand to Clorinda's lodge.

CHAPTER FIFTEEN
TROUBLE IS A GUY NAMED JOE

Bob felt good. There was no doubt in his mind that he was a lucky man to have Marian's love. He grinned and she returned a sedate smile. They stood at Clorinda's front door. Brass doorknocker in hand, Bob thumped it on the door, waited, and knocked again. "Maybe she's not at home? She had no idea I'd be back so soon. I guess people don't sit around in rockers waiting for me to call."

He stopped talking and listened intently. "Did you hear a sound a second ago from alongside the house?"

Marian walked along the porch until she reached the corner. She peered across a clearing thirty feet wide into a stand of white pines.

"Nothing, Bob."

Again, Bob rapped on the front door, a bit louder. A red squirrel jumped from the roof to a nearby birch. It chattered while scampering up the trunk. Had it made the sound he'd heard? The door opened.

"Bob and...," Clorinda said.

"Marian Alcott, soon to be Brunet," Marian said. She gave Bob a loving glance.

"I was in the kitchen drawing up a list of supplies to get from town. To what do I owe the pleasure of your visit?"

"We need your help, Clorinda. Marian needs a place to stay for a while."

"Oh," she said, smiling brightly. Her delight seemed exaggerated. Was it because Bob caught her unawares? "You're welcome to stay with me, Marian. I felt so bad when I read about what happened at your wedding. Come inside, both of you."

They followed her into the front room where a fire crackled in the great stone fireplace. It effectively served as a wall, separating the front room and the dining room.

"If you're hungry, I'll have Yvonne, the cook, whip something up for you."

"Thanks, but..."

"It's no trouble, Bob," Clorinda said, and bustled off to the kitchen.

While holding Marian's hand, he studied the oil painting above the fireplace. The gruff looking codger with the walrus mustache was Charlemagne Vinette, founder of the family fortune.

Bob's gaze continued to wander about the room until it lighted on a collection of guns in oak cases. At his urging, he and Marian walked to a gun case. An ivory handled .45 caliber revolver caught his eye. It was a single action "Frontier Model," but the carved ivory handles customized it.

Bob removed the revolver from its case and spun the cylinder. The gun was loaded. He put the revolver in the case when Clorinda returned.

She carried a large wooden tray heaped with homemade bread and sliced beef. A teapot steeped between the plates.

While placing the tray on a mahogany buffet, she said, "When you've finished eating, I'll show you to your room, Marian. Oh, the gun collection belonged to my father."

She left before either Bob or Marian could comment.

"Is she always so fidgety, Bob?"

"Maybe having a surprise guest ruffled her. Let's eat."

Hungry after their trek, Bob and Marian ravaged the platter of its cargo. Bob quickly demolished his sandwich and gulped down two cups of strong tea. He then rose to his feet and paced back and forth on the worn Persian rug.

Marian sat, chewing slowly as though savoring each bite. Her eyes flicked back and forth watching Bob preparing to leave.

When Clorinda returned, Marian jumped to her feet and gave Bob a hug and a long, lingering kiss. Bob pressed her to his chest. They fit together like two pieces of a jigsaw puzzle. With her arms around his neck, she stared without blinking into his eyes.

He stared at her face, memorizing each feature.

"Good-bye, Bob. I love you."

"I love you too. When you least expect it, I'll be back."

Marian smiled. "Write first so I'm able to fit you into my schedule."

Bob gave her a quizzical look before he caught on.

"Sorry, I couldn't resist. I feel good about us."

Reluctantly, Bob separated from Marian's warm embrace and shook Clorinda's hand. "Thanks for your help." He smiled. "The trust you have in me is gratifying, but there's lots yet to be done to clear myself."

Seeming not to hear Bob's words, Clorinda said, "Excuse me, I have to set that dratted clock."

She bustled off, this time into a room at the end of the front room and closed the door.

Without realizing that he was actually leaving, Bob found himself at the front door. He knew that talking was not going to get the job done, but action would. He kissed Marian one more time and hurried down the steps. He waved good by to her and smiled. Clorinda reappeared muttering something about good luck and waving.

He strode out of the yard. The sound of his footsteps on the packed ground set his soul free. Unhindered by any pack or person, he was at the command of the Manitou Hills. His senses were honed to receive the sights, sounds, and smells of his surroundings. Soon the weathered stone wall was behind him. The sound of his footsteps, of his breathing disappeared. Willingly, happily, he engulfed himself in the wilderness.

The report of a gun echoed through the hills. Bob stopped in his tracks, awakened to the presence of man. Probably one of his men hunting, he thought. It's a shame they had to resort to taking game illegally to fill their stomachs. He shrugged his broad shoulders.

After taking a moment to determine the direction from which the sound came, Bob plunged into and through a thicket. In a matter of thirty steps, he looked out over a small meadow at dry grasses swaying gently in the breeze. During a rainy spring, it was probably a marsh. He reconnoitered the clearing before stepping away from the brush.

He walked slowly looking for signs of life. At each step, he shifted his gaze from side to side. A red squirrel clattered up a tree. He saw no other movements. Sun hid behind clouds when he reached the center of the meadow. With each step, he grew more cautious. Where had the hunter gone? There was no doubt in his mind that the shot had come from the direction of the meadow. He whirled to look behind him.

When he faced forward again, he saw something across the meadow that he'd missed previously, a person slumped against a stump. Though Bob didn't recognize him at the distance, he somehow felt he knew his identity. Bob considered calling out, but decided to remain silent.

He continued his slow, measured steps until he was about fifty feet away. He recognized Joe Worman propped against the stump. A red blotch covered his chest. Even before reaching his side, Bob knew Joe was dead. A revolver lay next to his body, and Bob picked it up. It looked like Gil Quennel's Colt. Bob hunkered to examine Joe closely.

He felt a numbing blow on his head and saw a cascade of lights for an instant before everything went black.

The sun blinded him. His head throbbed. He couldn't move. Was he paralyzed? He could feel pain. A rope entwined him like a cocoon. The revolver he'd been examining was gone. What a dupe he'd been. Someone, probably the murderer, had conked him.

Straining at the ropes did no good. They creaked but didn't budge. His knife was still in its sheath, but he would have had to have been a contortionist to reach it. Bob thought of reasons why he had been trussed up instead of killed, but the more he thought about it the more his head throbbed.

The sound of leaves being crunched under foot caught his ear. If he had listened carefully before, he wouldn't be tied up. He scanned the screen of brush in front of him. No movement. With one foot, he pushed himself into a different position. His eyes widened. Striding toward him was Leo Long Mane.

"Thank God, I hope," he said.

"Bob! How the hell did you get yourself in this fix?"

"It was easy. I concentrated on Joe, and low and behold, I'm here."

Far from being a taciturn Indian, Leo talked rapidly as he sliced the ropes. "Who'd murder Mr. Worman? Looks like he's been sittin' there for a while. Looks like one shot did him in. Lucky I was in the neighborhood repairing Clorinda's stone bridge over the creek. We got to get out o' here. The sheriff could come anytime. Looks like you was set up for this. It took me a while to find you. This sure is a puzzler. There," he said cutting the last rope, "you're free."

Bob wobbled to his feet and clutched a small tree limb to steady himself. His head spun, or was the ground spinning?

Ed Pahnke

"Nobody's perfect," Bob said. He wanted to say something else, but he'd forgotten what he wanted to say.

Leo looked at him.

Bob looked at Leo.

Licking his lips, Bob said, "Every criminal forgets something." He squinted across the meadow. "Where does that path lead?"

"To another trail. I used that trail to get here. Are you feeling okay?"

While Leo talked, Bob examined the vicinity of the murder. Every time he stooped to inspect something, his dizziness returned, but he persisted. On the ground near the body, he found the case from a cartridge. Near the expended case, from between two tufts of grass, he extracted a plug of burnt pipe tobacco. He recalled that Joe smoked cigars. It seemed a cigar had always been stuck between his lips.

"This is dottle from a pipe, isn't it?" Bob asked.

"Dottle? Oh, tobacco. Smells like it," Leo said. "Some guy must've popped it from his pipe while standing here. I suppose a woman could o' done it, too, but not Miss Clorinda."

"She and Marian were at her house when I left," Bob said. "Let's go back there."

Bob wrapped the cartridge case and plug of tobacco in a piece of newspaper he had dug from his pocket. The two men tramped across the meadow, through the alders, and along the road to Clorinda Vinette's home.

Standing in the doorway, Marian waved and smiled.

"No need to knock on any doors," Bob said. "Marian must've seen us."

When they stood beside Marian on the porch, Bob introduced Leo to her, and they all walked into the house.

"Bob, I thought you were long gone." She glanced at Leo while she talked. "Clorinda's gone to town. She said she'd give you a lift if she saw you on the road. She had just disappeared down the road when I heard a shot. I thought of hunters at first, but the more I thought, the more I worried. After a while, I walked down the lane, but there was no sign of anyone. When I returned here, Yvonne was gone too."

She stepped closer to Bob. "What's that on your ear?"

She passed her hand along the side of his head. "Blood!" she said. "What happened?"

"The cut can wait."

"I'll see to that wound before you leave," she said.

With a few interruptions by Leo, Bob told the story of finding Joe's body.

"It seems like somebody intended to blame you for his murder," Marian said. "Too much coincidence to believe that, of all the times the shooting could occur, it happened when you walked by."

"How could anyone know you'd be here today, Bob?" Leo asked.

"Nat and Will knew, but they're back at camp. Even if they weren't, I trust them, but you were in the area repairing a stone bridge. I think maybe you were the target of the frame."

"I was planning to work on the bridge for the last week. I happened to pick today. Nobody but me knew when I'd be there."

Ed Pahnke

"I don't like all this talk. Frame up, hideout, murder. Where are we? This can't happen in our county. This isn't Chicago. We must speak with Clorinda."

"I agree, Marian," Bob said. "Clorinda may be able to shed some light on the mystery, but I think Leo and I'll take to the bush. Sweetheart, will you wait to hear Miss Clorinda's story?"

"Oh, no, you aren't leaving before I clean that wound and bandage it."

She turned to hunt for water and bandages and bumped into a chair. She faced Bob again, but appeared befuddled. "Don't you dare to go!"

Bob smiled after Marian left the room. He realized how nervous the situation had made her and how much he loved her. A wistful expression spread over his face.

Could they ever be together permanently? It had been bad enough to be labeled a thief, but now he'd be sought for murder too. He seemed to be in a hole so deep that he could never get out; but when he saw Marian enter the room carrying soap, a basin of water, and bandages, he resolved to fight even harder to prove his innocence.

CHAPTER SIXTEEN
A TALE FROM THE MANITOU HILLS

Time dragged, and the afternoon was almost gone before Marian heard the coughing and sputtering of a gasoline engine. A minute later, Clorinda's truck crawled up the rise on which the house was perched. Marian looked through the front window. Clorinda jumped from the cab. A cloud of smoke billowed about her head, obscuring her doeskin hat, but it didn't hide the apprehension lining her face.

She pushed open the door, her eyes widening when she saw Marian.

Without closing the door, she approached Marian and said, "Something's happened…" Her voice sputtered into silence, and her gaze shifted from side to side, never resting on Marian's face.

She began again. "I'm sorry to tell you. Your Bob murdered Joe Worman. I caught him kneeling over the body. Blood was puddled on Joe's chest. I was scared that he'd shoot me, too. He had a revolver in his hand,

and I had no choice. I grabbed a piece of wood, sneaked up behind him, and banged him on the head. Then, I ran to the truck, got some rope, and ran back. When I returned, he was still unconscious."

She cleared her throat. "When I finished tying him up, I wrapped the revolver in a cloth and drove to inform, tell Sheriff Blue what had happened. I found out from him that the gun belonged to Gil Quennel and that your Bob took it from Mister Quennel. It's in the police report I saw. After I signed a statement giving the facts, I led the sheriff and two deputies back to the clearing where I left Bob Brunet and the body.

"Right now, they're probably loading your Bob into one of their automobiles."

"I doubt that," Marian said. She smiled broadly.

Clorinda looked puzzled.

"Bob escaped. Leo Long Mane freed him. Both men are long gone. It seems as though Bob has some true friends."

Marian stared at Clorinda's face. Her gaze tried to catch Clorinda's eyes while she continued talking.

"What do you know about the murder, the true story?"

"Why, I. Nothing. I told you exactly what happened." She crossed her arms in front of her and clenched her fingers around her upper arms.

"As highly as you thought of Bob, or said you thought of him, I wonder why you didn't give him an opportunity to defend himself." She pointed her forefinger at Clorinda. The smile disappeared from her face. "What do you have to say now?"

Clorinda stammered and said, "I panicked. I saw Bob, the body, and the gun. I felt he would kill me if he saw me, and I don't have to say any more. This is my home. Please leave." She pressed her lips together, narrowing her eyes.

"Do you think you've heard the last of this? We're determined to learn the truth." Marian clenched her hands into fists and turned on her heel.

Instead of an open door, Marian faced Roland Blue.

He loomed over her. "Where the hell is Brunet?" Dressed in black, the sheriff appeared even more ferocious, glaring down at Marian.

Marian was not about to quake and quail before Alice Blue's father. "Mister Blue, don't try to bully me. Bob is innocent." She was about to add that she thought the sheriff was guilty of more transgressions than Bob, but decided such an accusation would add to her woes. "I don't know where Bob went, but I do know he'll work tirelessly to prove he's innocent."

"You're under arrest for being an accessory after the fact".

Clorinda smiled a relieved sort of smile.

Marian stuck her chin out. "Do I get the rubber hose treatment? Are you going to put handcuffs on my wrists? I've told you all I know."

"Miss Marian, I'm not going to take any guff from you. Bob Brunet is a bad apple, and I'll catch up with him and lock him up permanent."

"You can try," Marian said. "Now, do you intend to arrest me? If so, the entire county will know you've taken out your spite on me because Bob continues to elude you."

The expression on Roland Blue's face became less resolute, his complexion remaining florid. "I'll be watching you. I don't have a case against you, yet. But don't think because you're a woman I won't throw you in the hoosegow when I can prove you're helping Brunet."

"Thank you for your warning. I don't think you're a bad man, only misguided. Perhaps one day we may even become friends.

"Please stand aside." Roland Blue moved, and Marian walked out of the house.

Marian took a deep breath. She thought Bob would have been proud of her, and she felt proud of herself. In front of her lay the forested Manitou Hills. Behind the trees, streaks of red and purple ushered in twilight. She clenched her haversack, and marched out onto the forest road. Where could she go? Uncertain about the location of Bob's camp, she tried to remember.

She jumped when Roland Blue tapped her on her shoulder with his hand.

"I know we're on different sides, but I can't leave you stranded here in the middle of the wilderness. It'll be dark soon, and I'm heading back to Vinette, anyway. Let me give you a ride there?"

Marian hesitated. Perhaps Mister Blue did believe in what he was doing. After all, he was her best friend's father. She smiled to herself. A ride would be welcome.

"Very well. Thank you, Sheriff Blue."

Where would she go? Perhaps the room in the Church at the Corners could provide temporary shelter.

CHAPTER SEVENTEEN
MEETING MISTER INSIDE

The north wind blew a fine drizzle against the white clapboard Church at the Corners. The sun had not appeared from behind a blanket of iron gray clouds all that Sunday.

Bob and Will crouched behind a clump of birches, rain forming brooklets on their wool coats and caps. Bob tried to focus in on the church with a pair of rusty binoculars borrowed from one of his men, but mist kept clouding the lenses.

"That guy is in the warm, snug church while we freeze our asses off on this miserable day," Will said. "What are we waiting for? Do you think somebody is peeking out at us from the church? You're too cautious, Bob."

"Okay. Stop your carping. Let's go inside to meet Dick Legh."

"Carping is it? I should let you go inside by yourself. Better yet, I should go inside by myself."

"Everything seems quiet," Bob said. "Let's go."

"About time," Will said, his brows knit together. "Mike did say the church would be empty."

After a long wait in a cramped position, Bob smiled when he stretched and straightened himself. He and Will hurried across the parking lot, past a solitary black flivver, and up the steps.

There were no lights on inside. The nave was quiet but warm, and warm air drifted through the registers from a hot air furnace.

"Hot damn," Will said and hastily added, "sorry God. I think I'll settle down by a hot air register while you and Dick Legh talk."

The mayor sat in a front row pew.

"Let's both meet him. I don't want to have to repeat what he says."

"I'm coming." He dragged out the words.

When Bob sidled along the front pew. Will followed him to where Dick Legh waited.

Wide-eyed as always, Dick Legh's moon face had the appearance of an owl's. He stood, smiled a genuine smile, and shook Bob's and Will's hands, simultaneously, obviously in a hurry. His hands were sweaty, and he rubbed them on his gray Norfolk Jacket. Knowing he was consorting with a fugitive probably made him uncomfortable.

He wasted no time commenting on the weather or trivial matters. "Bob, I have a favor to ask of you, and I may have some information to help your cause. Besides being the mayor of Vinette, I was on the Board of Directors of the King Bank, and I had access to information about Richard King and his bank.

"I'm in desperate straits. I have only enough cash to keep the wolf from the door." He paused as though wondering what to say next. Looking Bob in the eye, he said, "There's this loan. I owe money to the King Bank, and John King wants payment. If I don't pay by Friday, he'll take everything I own. I put it all up for collateral. Also, I need money to run a respectable campaign against Gil Quennel's crony, Everett Ivers, for District Attorney. The November election isn't too far off. If I can win and get an honest person to run for sheriff, we can go a long way toward preventing the good folks from being victimized."

A thoughtful look on his face, Bob stroked his chin and let his index finger rest in his dimple. At the same time, Will was pulling on his left ear. If a baseball game were in progress, there would have been no doubt the two men were signaling game strategy. Indeed, they were determining what to do.

"How much do you need, Dick?"

"Five hundred will save the property and finance the election."

"I don't have it with me, but we can raise the money and let you have it. When can you repay?"

"Six months, if things go well in the election."

"My men and I will throw our support to you, and I know of a fellow who fits the bill for sheriff, Calvin Little. He's on the ballot as an independent right now. Can you support him?"

"The peddler? Everybody knows him, but what's his background?"

"He was a deputy for a couple of years. With our support he'll have a chance, and I'm sure he'll agree." Bob changed the subject. "You mentioned that you can supply us with inside information about the King Bank?"

"Yes, I can from the time when Richard King was running the bank. John King forced me out at the same time he gave me notice he wasn't going to renew my loans. John King wants me to look bad so he can keep me out of all public offices.

"I can tell you this, too. The bank was barely holding its own when Richard was president. With so many loans defaulting, the bank's income was drying up. If Richard King had foreclosed on properties, he would have been stuck with them. He was no friend of Quennel's. John King added his own capital when he took over, and he has money coming in when Quennel buys properties. Then he lends money to Quennel. Why Quennel wants all that land is beyond me."

"Would we possibly find anything incriminating by visiting the bank after hours?" Bob asked.

"Try the file cabinets in John King's office, his desk too. I don't think you want to try the vault." Dick fished around in his coat pocket. "This key will open the side door, unless John had the lock changed. I had crazy thoughts of using it to steal my notes back.

"Anyway, try the side door, but please make it look like the lock's been picked. Richard gave the key to me years ago, but I've never used it. If you're interested in financial statements, try the bookkeeper's office. It's down the hall from John's office. You're daring. If you give it a try, good luck."

"At this point, I've no choice. I have to be daring," Bob said.

Dick Legh rose. "I'll be going, and if you have no objections, I'd like to leave first. I can't afford to be considered your associate much less be seen with you, but I give you my word that I'll do everything in my power to exonerate you."

"We understand," Bob said. "Cal Little will deliver an envelope to you. Nothing to sign. Your word to repay is good enough."

"Thanks. I have to pay off the loans by Friday."

Before Dick left, they again shook hands, this time to seal the agreement.

When Dick Legh had gone, Bob said, "We'll wait half an hour. That should give Dick plenty of time to be elsewhere." Bob checked his pocket watch.

Will craned his neck to see the watch. "Supper will be cold by the time we get there." His stomach growled in discontent.

Another sound reached Bob's ears, that of feet padding down steps. Bob regularly carried the twenty-two he had brought from home. It didn't have much stopping power unless it hit a vital area. However, Bob was marksman enough to get good use from it. He spun around on the seat.

Marian stood at the foot of the stairs.

"Bob," she said. "And Will too."

Bob leaped over the back of the pew and into the aisle. Marian ran down the aisle into his arms. Will coughed politely.

"I changed to this dress when I saw you. I was wearing pajamas. I'm staying here until I can get my money from the bank. I intend to be an independent woman for a while. There, all the questions about me are answered."

They embraced for a moment.

She quickly told Bob and Will what Clorinda had said to her. When Marian finished, she asked, "Has the cut healed? Are you all right?"

"I'm fine, but if I keep accumulating charges, I might make the most wanted list. For your safety and ours too, we have to leave."

"You always seem to be leaving."

"A kiss before we leave?" Will asked. "I might as well benefit from this meeting."

Marian obliged by planting a kiss on each of Will's cheeks. She and Bob walked back up the aisle hand in hand. Bob touched the gold wedding band tucked safely in his coat pocket. They turned toward each other and embraced.

Moments later Bob and Will trudged through the cold drizzle. Marian's warmth slowly dimmed to a memory.

CHAPTER EIGHTEEN
ARRESTING FACTS

Bob and Leo stood at the entrance to the gangway between King's Mercantile Bank and the dry goods store. Bob had buttoned his coat against the frosty night, the first such night in October. The heavens were alive with flecks of light, but in the gangway, the only light came from a light bulb over the side entrance to the bank.

Before entering the gangway, Bob glanced up and down the street. It appeared as if he and Leo were the only ones out that night. As a signal, Bob nodded and Leo Long Mane jumped into the gangway. After the initial leap, they walked stealthily to the door.

The key held tightly in his hand, Bob reached out for the door. The key, moist from his perspiration, slid easily into the keyhole. Turning it in the lock, he pushed the door open without making a sound.

He rubbed his sweaty palms on his trousers and cast furtive glances up and down the gangway before entering the bank. Leo followed. After removing the key from the lock, Bob swung the door shut. Bob and Leo had officially broken into a bank. Bob was familiar with the bank lobby, but Leo had never seen the inside of a bank. They walked carefully until their eyes became accustomed to the dark. A dim light glowed in the lobby, but their destination was in the back offices.

Bob nudged Leo. "It's safe to light the lantern."

"I don't know why you had me to come along. I can't read."

"The men are used to Will. They'll follow his orders in case of trouble. I need a dependable person to carry the lantern and listen for Will's knock. You've proved that your hearing is keen. If you hear a knock, douse the light, but for now, light the lantern."

Leo grappled with the lantern before igniting the wick.

Bob had stationed Will outside as a lookout. Since it could be vital that he and the men recognized each other, they all wore forest-green Filson Cruisers. Trips to the movies made Bob aware gloves were required attire for all criminal deeds. A scant half-mile away, seven of Bob's men waited. They probably hoped they'd not be called because if they were, it would mean trouble. Bob wanted enough men on hand to be able to cause a diversionary ruckus while he and Leo disappeared into the night.

Bob pulled his black slouch hat down over his ears, and Leo copied his lead with a similar style hat, his only one.

Leo raised the lantern above his head and walked ahead of Bob along the hallway.

Bob tapped him on his shoulder and pointed to the door. He said, "This is the president's office."

Northern Knights

"Hoover has an office here?"

"No," Bob said, suppressing a smile. Then again, after the up coming election Hoover could have such an office, Bob reasoned. "It's John King's office. He's president of the bank. See if the door is unlocked."

Leo pushed the door open and shined the light from the lantern inside. There were no outside windows in the office.

Bob was prepared to knock the locks off any desks or file cabinets with a hammer and punch. Optimistic and realistic at the same time, he hoped to find something, anything, which would explain why King and Quennel were grabbing land. Before unpacking his hardware, he pulled on a drawer handle. The drawer of the file cabinet resisted. Bob aimed the hammer at the punch and hit it.

The lock separated from the oak drawer. Meanwhile, Leo jiggled the drawers at John King's desk. They too were locked.

"Do you want to start here?" Leo asked. He snapped the lock open using the blade of his hunting knife.

"Over here with the lantern, Leo."

"So, you want to start over there."

He walked over to where Bob stood and directed the light from the lantern on the contents of the open drawer. Bob thumbed through the files. Finding nothing pertinent, he punched open another drawer then another in a hurried search for evidence.

"Bob, is that a map of Gamwell County?"

Bob looked up, stared at the map tacked onto the wall and said, "Yes."

He would have dived back into the files, but Leo again asked, "What's the meaning of all those little colored squares along the river? That is the river, ain't it?"

A bit peeved at the interruption, Bob again looked at the map, this time more closely. He said, "Sometimes we miss what's right in front of our noses. Those squares represent parcels of land owned by Gil Quennel. Most of them are bunched up around the fork of the Moose Ear River. Those sons o' bitches have already added my property to their holdings. Now, why the hell would they want to surround the river? When we find the reason, we may be close to solving the mystery."

He continued his search through the drawers. When he finished, Leo said, "Don't forget John King's desk. "

"I hope we find something there," Bob said. They walked across the oak floor and then the carpet in the center of the office, stopping behind the sprung desk drawer. Bob quickly sorted through the cluttered desk drawer until he found a partnership agreement between John King and Gil Quennel. Before continuing, he put a carbon copy of the document in his inside coat pocket, hoping John King wouldn't notice it was missing. Then he closed the drawer.

Moments later, he puzzled over six sheets of paper. "Now here are a half a dozen payments totaling nearly a thousand dollars to Elliot Bevis. There's no reason for these to be here. They should be in with expense invoices. In your travels, have you ever heard of this fellow?"

Leo shook his head.

"I think I'll take one invoice from this file." He folded the paper and stuffed it into his inside coat pocket, too. There seemed to be nothing else unusual about the contents in the rest of the desk drawers.

"I think we've finished here. Let's go into the Bookkeeping Department."

Two fire retardant record tubs made of sheet steel and painted gray stood in the center of the Bookkeeping Department. The tubs were on wheels so that they could be rolled out of the bank in case of fire. Bob was certain they would contain loan account files or General Ledger files. After breaking one lock, Bob found which tub contained loan files. Most of the people in the county had loans, but how many would be able to repay them?

Starting at the back of the file, he looked through the closed loans. Joe Worman had paid off his loan before John King took over, but where had he gotten three hundred and fifty dollars? Dick Legh's loan was in a section reserved for loans about to be called. Bob smiled. John King was going to be surprised. Looking at the location of Dick's property, he noted it was not near the Moose Ear River. A ledger sheet showed a thousand dollar unsecured loan was outstanding to Richard King, but Bob could not see John King pressing Richard's wife for payment.

Bob thumped the sliding door of the tub closed.

"Let's go, Leo," Bob said.

Except for broken locks, the room looked as it had before the two men entered. They headed toward the side door. On the way, they turned up their coat collars against possible recognition. Bob smiled. Who would be outdoors at that time of night? After opening the door, he paused. He scratched the lock with a penknife blade to make it look as though it had been jimmied. When he closed the door behind him and Leo, he thought that the meanings of the words in life were a matter of points of view. The same door was both entrance and exit. Bob thought of Gil Quennel as bad, but Quennel thought of himself as good.

Points of view stuck in Bob's mind while he and Leo kept to the shadows in the gangway. While walking, he wondered where had Will gone? Maybe he waited for them on Main Street.

Headlights shined on Bob and Leo, but Bob didn't feel happy as he had when he was surprised at his twenty-first birthday. Alarm described his feeling when he shielded his eyes from the glare of the headlights.

"Up with your hands!" Roland Blue shouted. Bob recognized the sheriff's voice.

"Oh God," Leo whispered, more to himself than to Bob. He froze on the spot.

Bob saw three shadows behind the headlights. Had Will been captured? Bob had thoughts of a mad dash to freedom or kingdom come. His dreams of liberating the county were just that, dreams. He clenched his fists in frustrated anger.

"What do we do?" asked Leo.

Bob felt he had to think of an answer. "When I lay my hand on your shoulder, hit the ground," Bob whispered. "Then crawl like hell for the gangway. I think…"

The sound of loud voices reached Bob's ears, a jumble of words. Feet shuffled over the brick-street. Trying to see over the glare of the headlights, Bob saw a bumpy, moving shadow that undulated like a ten-foot inchworm.

The black shape grew when it closed the distance between itself and the sheriff's automobiles.

"What the hell are you two yahoos waiting for?" the sheriff shouted at Bob and Leo. "Throw up your hands."

Bob and Leo obeyed.

"Watch those bandits, boys, I'm going to find out who's coming."

One of the shapes behind the sheriff's blockade disengaged himself from the others. Bulky enough to be Roland Blue, he strode toward the commotion. By that time, Bob could see individual shapes moving in on them.

The sound of voices and shuffling continued until Roland Blue said in a course voice, "Who the hell is that?"

The sounds didn't waver, nor was there an answer.

"Stop, damn you, stop," Blue's voice said from the shadows.

A tribe of folks wearing forest-green coats passed between Bob and Leo and their adversaries.

"Get the hell out of the way," Sheriff Blue, shouted.

A shot rang out. Blue was not stingy with bullets.

"What?" Voices said from the crowd.

The crowd scattered in seeming disarray right between the three automobiles whose lights shined on Bob and Leo.

Leo didn't move when Bob touched his shoulder, so Bob grabbed hold of his coat and dragged him in the direction from which the angels had come. He thought of the intruders as angels. Bob and Leo had to be fast before the diversion disappeared. Leo grasped the idea quickly and sped away in front of Bob. Thoughts of defeat were replaced by a daring escape. They ran. Bob's lips parted, his hungry lungs demanding more air, boots clattering on the brick street. In the background, Bob heard shouts from the turmoil.

He took a quick look over his shoulder and immediately bumped into Leo. Both men fell to the street.

"Get up, Leo," Bob said, and jumped up.

Leo scrambled to his feet. Bob knew they had to get off the main street before Roland Blue got after them in his automobile. Bob looked toward the corner of the block. If they could get there before the sheriff and his men could resume pursuit, he and Leo could disappear into the night.

"Turn left at the end of the block, Leo, but stick close to me."

They dashed toward the end of the block, past one darkened store after another. They reached the last store on the block, when headlights shined on them. Their shadows spread out in front of them.

"There they are," shouted a voice. "Stop or I shoot!"

"Don't stop," Bob yelled.

"I'm not. I've got to be free. Remind me never to go on a bank job with you again." Leo gasped for breath.

A shot rang out from behind them sending a bullet biting into a clapboard wall. A shower of slivers pelted Bob.

"You okay?" Leo asked.

"Don't slow down, Leo."

He heard the sound of a revving automobile engine.

"We can't outrun a flivver," Bob said, puffing. "We have to hide."

They skidded around the corner. No lights glimmered on Lumber Street. Two rows of small shops stretched two hundred feet in the direction of the alley.

"Run across the street and into the alley," Bob said, "We've got to find a place to hide."

The two men dashed across the street and into the alley. Mounds of crates and lines of garbage cans were black outlines in the darkness. They filled the narrow gravel covered road where Bob and Leo ran, their feet crunching on the surface. The sounds of his own breathing filled his ears. In front of them, a searchlight glared, dilating Bob's pupils.

"There they are," a voice said.

Another voice shouted, "You're under arrest."

"Over here," yet another voice said from behind them.

Bob turned, but he saw nothing.

"Back this way before you get killed," a husky voice whispered.

The voice sounded familiar to Bob.

"Who the hell are you?" Leo asked.

"I can't show myself. They'll catch on and drive into the alley. Flatten against the fence. Edge to the corner. I got a flivver waiting."

Bob figured that he had no choice but to trust the unseen person. "Follow me, Leo." He pushed behind crates and cans and sidled along the fence that ran along the alley. Leo followed.

"Where did they go?" A voice from behind the searchlight said. The light scanned the alley.

"Drive down the alley. We'll find 'em and arrest 'em."

The glare from headlights filled the alley when Bob and Leo arrived at the corner.

"Over here. It's me. Will."

Bob and Leo dashed to the black automobile with its engine running.

"Will," Bob said. "Thank God. You saved our biscuits from burning this time for sure."

"This ain't the first time, or the last," Will added.

"Come on, Leo," Bob said. "The getaway car awaits. Where'd you get the car?"

"Borrowed it."

They scrambled into the automobile. Will threw it in gear, and they roared away from the Vinette business district and into the countryside. Nobody spoke.

Thankful they had escaped, Bob wondered what his findings at the bank meant. Each scrap seemed to shroud answers more than answer questions. In fact, every step he took seemed to be a backward step putting him deeper into his forest hideout. Though life in the woods suited him, he wanted to be free to walk in society with his head up. John King and Gil Quennel were free to do as they pleased, continuing their control of Gamwell County; and there wasn't even a whisper of a clue to Richard King's whereabouts.

Bob drove his fist into the palm of his hand. Damn it, he said under his breath, if I'm discouraged, I'll drag everyone else down in the dumps with me.

"Well," Bob said, "things have got to get better.

"Why?" Will said.

Leo tried to smile but said nothing. They continued toward the Manitou Hills.

CHAPTER NINETTEN
THE NEWS OF THE DAY

A day had elapsed since Bob's nighttime foray into the King Bank.

Seated at a square maple table in her room, Marian studied the Vinette Weekly Journal. Her ladder backed chair creaked each time she moved. She had time for toast and coffee before beginning her new job. It was not the teaching position she so loved, but it was a job. She would be clerking at Wharton's Dry Goods Store in downtown Vinette. Another eager miss had snapped up the teaching position.

Estranged from her father, Marian had rented a room from the Darcy's. Their boarding house was clean. The room was small but neat and airy, a nice place to read and sip tea or coffee in peace.

Withdrawing her money from the bank was no a problem. The problem arose at her home. She'd had a room full of clothing, but to get her things, she had had to brave her father's wrath. After a few practice blusters, she had been ready for a scene.

She simply walked into her home. Her father ranted and raved the whole time she was there. Outwardly, she ignored him, but inwardly, she cried. She packed blankets, pillowcases, and sheets into one valise, clothing into another. Her tattered Raggedy Ann doll was packed carefully with her clothes. Her father had been red with anger when she left. He'd forget, but would Marian?

Every moment Marian was not on the job, she worked for Bob. Her eyes and ears were added to those of Calvin Little finding bits information that could be helpful to him. Her successes were rare and questionable.

At about the time Bob was to have stolen Gil Quennel's cattle, a truck had been seen in the middle of the night at the Quennel farm. Al Sharp had been jacklighting deer that night. He had said he saw a truck. Marian didn't approve of Al's technique, but information was information. The truck's tires had dug more deeply leaving Quennel's property than they had entering it.

Deputy Galton had said the writing on the ransom notes has changed. The writing appeared to be a hurried scrawl on the last note. Of what significance, if any, these bits of fact were, Marian didn't know. However, she wrote everything in her journal.

With the election a mere month away, she planned to campaign for the "Clean Slate" of candidates. She was not interested in electioneering for her favorite, Philip LaFollette for Wisconsin governor because he didn't need her help. Who would vote for that old Democrat Albert G. Schmedeman for governor against him? Her interest centered on Gamwell County. She worked for Cal Little for Sheriff and Dick Legh for District Attorney.

Her vote for president would go to Franklin D. Roosevelt. The sound of his words gave her confidence. Although she had finished her coffee, Marian lingered reading her newspaper, but it didn't contain political doings of interest to those in the county. Instead, this time the headlines announced murder and mayhem in the worst tradition of big city yellow journalism:

BOLD BANK BANDITS ESCAPE CAPTURE

Bank bandits eluded Sheriff Blue after a running gun battle in the streets of Vinette late Thursday night. The identity of the desperados is as yet unknown. A spokesman for the Sheriff's Department praised the alarm system for alerting the sheriff and two deputies to the forced entry.

Mr. John King, the bank's president, reported that two hundred dollars and sundry papers were missing from a locked drawer in the Bookkeeping Department.

Descriptions of the two bandits are sketchy at best. It is believed that two men dressed in dark coats and slouch hats are guilty of the crime.

Sheriff Roland Blue blames a mob of drunken citizens for the bandits' escape. The mob got between the sheriff and the robbers. He declines further statement.

Nothing has been seen of the robbers since the night of the crime.

PROMINENT LOCAL WOMAN MURDERED IN HER HOME

Clorinda Vinette was shot to death in her Manitou Hills estate late Thursday night. Granddaughter of Charlemagne Vinette, Miss Clorinda was the last Vinette living in Gamwell County.

She was found early Friday morning by her cook, Yolanda Irons. Mrs. Irons had been at her home overnight. Miss Clorinda had been shot with a .45 caliber single action revolver. The weapon appeared to have been part of a collection owned by Miss Clorinda. It was left in the house by the murderer.

Sheriff Roland Blue is looking for Bob Brunet, a local outlaw, in connection with the killing…

Marian threw down the newspaper in disgust. She remembered Bob had handled a revolver when he and she were in Clorinda's home. Could it be a coincidence, or had somebody been watching them? If it would have done any good, she would have called the newspaper and defended Bob. She retrieved the newspaper and continued to read.

Miss Vinette had recently caught Bob Brunet after he had allegedly murdered Joe Worman. Because of the accusations, there is believed to have been bad blood between Bob Brunet and Clorinda Vinette.

Fingerprints found on the revolver that killed Miss Vinette are being matched with those found on the weapon that killed Joe Worman.

Marian stopped reading and gazed out the window. Her spirits dropped. Why should Bob be running into all this bad luck now? She felt certain the gun he'd examined was the same one that had killed Clorinda.

But Bob had an unshakeable alibi, and the irony of it curved Marian's lips into a joyless smile. Bob had to admit to a robbery for which he was not suspected to clear himself of a murder for which he was being sought. The sheriff could vouch for Bob's whereabouts.

A quick glance at the clock on the wall told her she had to start her workday. She dropped the newspaper on the table. When she closed the door behind her, she shook her head again. So much for relaxing with the newspaper.

CHAPTER TWENTY
THE CLEAN SLATE

Wind rattled the window sashes and whistled around the panes-of-glass. Her eyes closed, Marian pulled the bed covers over her ears, trying to ignore the alarm clock that ticked next to her bed. Night had not yet given up its hold to light of day, but Marian grudgingly opened one eye to squint at the clock. Five minutes past five o'clock in the morning. Who would ever arise at such an hour? She would.

She had to shepherd voters. Throwing off the covers, she sat on the edge of the bed and wiggled her feet around on the cold floor, searching for her slippers. Each time her bare feet touched the cold linoleum, it sent a series of goose bumps dancing over her skin. She found one furry slipper.

She refused to hop about on one foot looking for a slipper. Bending over, she peered into the darkness under her bed. She saw a lump and reached her hand toward it. If it moved she knew she'd scream. She grasped the other furry slipper.

After putting it on her right foot, she stood, gathered her flannel nightgown around her, and scuffed toward the kerosene stove. The room felt like an icebox. She shivered. With the exception of a spot in the center, the windowpanes were frosted over. She fumbled for matches on the table, lit the stove, and waited.

At the first hint of heat, she shed her nightgown. All of her clothes were stacked on a chair, underwear on top. She hopped into her panties and fitted her brassiere over her breasts. The garments felt like cold steel on her skin while she dressed.

In twenty minutes, she had eaten and completed her toilet. Marian was to meet the Clean Slate candidates and poll watchers at the Palace Restaurant. She had decided to skip a lengthy breakfast. After buttoning her forest-green Filson Cruiser securely around her neck, she tiptoed out of the room and down the steps.

A brisk wind pushed dark gray clouds across the northern sky. A few dry leaves clattered along the sidewalk while Marian hurried to the meeting place.

She arrived at the well-lighted restaurant before six. In contrast, the surrounding store windows were black. When she entered the restaurant, sounds of rattling silverware and murmuring voices greeted her. What she saw made her wonder if it were possible to ever have peace in Gamwell County.

Except for a row of empty tables down the center of the restaurant, each high-backed booth hosted five or six people. She recognized many of those on the north side of the dining room as her friends. On the south side of the room, Roland Blue and Gil Quennel sat surrounded by their retainers.

Blue, wearing a black balmacaan, and Quennel, a sporty coat with a beaver collar, talked in animated fashion. Burly people scurried about them, but nobody crossed into the center, no man's land, between the two forces. Even the waiters skirted the line.

Marian waded through the crowd looking for Cal Little and Dick Legh. Waiters pranced about, ducking and stretching; trays were heaped with bacon, eggs, and pancakes. There were no smiles while the people stuffed food into their mouths. Judging from the gruff expressions on the faces of the men, Marian felt that a wrong word or gesture would certainly bring on a brawl. They all seemed to be flexing their muscles while eating.

"Good morning." Marian smiled, cheeks rosy from the raw, cold morning air.

Expressionless faces turned toward her. Plates cleaned of food cluttered the table.

When Dick Legh recognized her, he doffed his slouch hat and smiled. Marian considered it to be a smile, but it looked more like he had swallowed castor oil. Dick, Cal Little, and a lean man clad in a Filson Cruiser stood. Cal pulled a chair toward the booth for Marian. During the campaign, she had gotten used to seeing a red and blue tie flapping on his chest. While she waited to be seated, she glanced across the empty boundary line at Gil Quennel. He had been devouring her with his eyes. His eyes were like hands touching her, and his lips curved into a mock smile. Cal placed a chair behind Marian. Sitting down on the wooden chair, she turned her back to Gil Quennel.

"I'm ready for an honest election and a resounding victory," Marian said.

The men nodded. The smell of fried bacon and cigarette smoke filled her nostrils. What enjoyment was there in puffing smoke?

Cal expelled a large cloud of smoke from his mouth before replacing his pipe in his mouth. "It looks like trouble is brewing. Those fellows," (He inclined his head toward Quennel and company.) "appear to want to control the polls with force. If we let 'em push voters around, me and Dick…"

"Dick and I," Marian corrected him.

Cal smiled before he continued, "We'll loose for sure. We've got to drop a man off at each polling place by the time the polls open at seven." He quickly added, "and you too, Miss Marian. That'll make them thin down their forces. There'll be less chance of fights with one on one."

"Don't fret about me, Cal," Marian said. "I don't carry a vinaigrette or a fan to revive myself should I feel faint. I'm able to fend for myself."

Cal nodded without changing his concerned expression.

"How do we get everybody to the polls?" the lean man asked. "Most of us don't have automobiles."

"Hitch rides with those who have," Cal said. "Nat Mutch is borrowing a truck from Clorinda Vinette."

Shocked, Marian stared at Cal.

"She won't be using it no more. The question is: do we supply the men with clubs now to show we won't be pushed around?"

Dick Legh cleared his throat. "Nat had better stay out of sight. Blue knows him from when Nat and Bob withdrew money from the bank." He took a gulp of coffee. "We don't want violence, if it can be avoided. Pass out the 'walking sticks.' The men and Miss Marian should be prepared for the worst."

"I don't think I'll have to resort to physical force," Marian said. "I'll confront any offender as I would a child in one of my classes." She wondered if she was being naive.

"I think Marian has the right outlook on this election," Dick said. "Talk first."

"When do we start for the polls?" the lean man asked and scratched his whiskers.

Marian had the same question on her mind, and she looked at Dick, then Cal for answers.

While they talked, one of Bob's men walked toward the exit. He cut across the centerline. A husky fellow from Quennel's force challenged him. They stood chest to chest. Their hands clenched into fists, glaring into each other's eyes. Neither spoke.

Cal stood quickly but not quietly. He tipped over a chair. It clattered onto the linoleum-covered floor. He thumped his walking stick on the wooden table. Dishes and cups rattled. Everybody fell silent, and looked at the two men in the neutral zone.

"Come here, Virgil," Cal said. "No trouble. We want an honest election, not fist fights." The man in the Filson Cruiser backed away.

Roland Blue stood. "Follow me outside, men. If we want to guide the voters, we've got to be at the polls."

Blue's statement was followed by a round of chuckles and applause from their side. They stood, ready to follow Quennel outside.

In a few minutes, only the people siding with Cal and Dick remained in the restaurant.

"Why are we letting them get ahead of us?" the lean man asked.

"He's right. We've waited long enough for Nat Mutch," Dick said.

"There ain't enough automobiles for everybody," Cal said. "We have no choice."

"Some people will be able to ride to their posts," Marian said. "Others can walk."

Cal, still standing, shook his walking stick as a signal to leave. The men and Marian followed him to the front door. When Marian passed Griffon Sloan, the owner of the Palace Restaurant, she noted the relieved expression on his face. There had been a real danger of a full-scale battle in his restaurant.

Outside, the clouds at the horizon were tinged with red. A stiff breeze blew from the east.

Owners of automobiles waited inside their vehicles. Those without transportation scurried about looking for room to squeeze into automobiles. Marian decided to wait for the truck and Nat Mutch.

She didn't have long to wait. A black Ford truck chugged along the red brick street toward her and pulled alongside the curb. Nat smiled at her from behind the wheel.

Marian, Cal, and Dick walked to the side of the truck.

Northern Knights

"Sorry I'm late. I've been watching from down the street." He pointed back along the street. "I wanted the sheriff to leave before I got here."

"A wise precaution," Dick Legh said. "Now, Miss Marian and those two fellows need a ride to the polls. Take them all to Langston. There are three polls there. Come back here when you've finished, and the three of us will scout around the county."

Marian sat next to Nat in the front seat. "How is Bob?" she asked.

"Everybody in camp is fine, but Bob has changed, somehow. He's not as cheerful as he was when I first met him, but we all hope for the best in the election. A win for our side could mean we return to our homes soon."

Marian smiled. She hoped for the best too, but she was concerned about Bob. Would the ordeal change him? She loved him the way he was, but she put the thoughts out of her mind and concentrated on her role in the election.

"Thank you for the ride, Mr. Mutch." Marian said. A barbershop served as a polling place. A line of potted plants stood behind large glass windows, and a lone barber, probably trying to take advantage crowds of people, had opened early to cut hair. Voting booths were constructed of cardboard.

Marian's assignment was to wait outside and watch for problems. She planned to ask questions of some voters when they arrived or departed. Were they coerced into voting for any particular candidate? Still she knew that she would have to watch for Quennel's men.

With each breath, she billowed clouds about her face. She stamped her feet to warm them. Overhead, patches of blue had appeared in the sky. The bruiser Quennel assigned to the poll paced back and forth on the sidewalk. He stopped a man and a woman, and the couple shook their heads. The bruiser laid his hand on the man's shoulder. The woman took hold of the man's hand and tried to drag him away, but the bruiser let fly a right hand that hit the man on his nose.

"Stop that," Marian yelled. Cold was forgotten. She rushed to where the three people stood. "You have no right to punch anyone."

She shook her finger at the bully.

"Who the hell are you?" he asked.

"I am Marian Alcott. What's your name?"

"I ain't got no name. I'm here to learn people how to vote, not play games with no woman."

Marian looked at the bruiser's face. He had a boulder jaw and no forehead. He squinted down at her.

"Do you know you can be thrown into jail for assaulting people?"

The bruiser smiled and said, "He ain't hurt." He turned to the man and woman standing on the sidewalk. "Are you?" He thumped the man on the back and forced a smile.

"No, he didn't hurt me," the man said. The woman nodded her head affirming his statement.

Marian said, "If this bully gets away with influencing you, he'll force others to vote his way. Our homes and lives will continue to be ruled by might not right."

The man cleared his throat. Without looking at Marian, he said, "Let's go in and vote, Honey, and get away from this busybody."

Northern Knights

Marian fumed while they walked into the barbershop. Try to help some people and get slapped in the face for your trouble. Inside the barbershop, a judge hovered over the couple's shoulders trying to see their ballots while they voted. He succeeded and shook his head. The signal put a smile on the bruiser's face.

If Marian had no better luck with the voters that followed, there would be little hope the reformers could carry the precinct. She searched her brain for a solution. Getting rid of the bruiser would be the ideal situation. Thwarting his efforts to intimidate would solve the problem, too.

The bruiser walked away. Marian followed him. She stood in front of him as an old man approached the barbershop.

"Good morning," she said. "It's a good day for an honest election."

The bruiser tried to circle around her. She out maneuvered him. The old man went into the barbershop. When a judge tried to watch him, he shooed him away.

The bruiser's smile vanished, and he glared at Marian. "If you don't get the hell out o' here, lady…"

"Will you hit a woman?" Marian asked. "That won't look good. I'll call the Langston police officer. He'll arrest you for assaulting a woman."

The bruiser grabbed Marian by her waist and began to carry her toward an automobile. Marian flailed her arms and kicked her feet, to no avail.

"Help! Help!"

"Damn it. Shut your mouth."

He tried to put his hand over her mouth, but she wiggled free and stood on the street. He lunged at her. She dodged from his grasp. He lunged again. Like a will-o'-the-wisp, she was gone. She yelled again. "Help! Help!"

People emerged from nearby houses and surrounded Marian and the bruiser. His eyes shifted from side to side. His face reddened from anger.

"I want this man arrested," Marian said.

"I'll get Sam," a young woman said. Skirts flying, she dashed toward the filling station.

For his part, the bruiser lumbered toward a black touring car. The circle of people parted when he left, and nobody tried to detain him. He didn't return.

Marian spent the rest of the day shaking hands with voters and accepting congratulations. Her hands and feet froze, but her heart was stoked by success.

CHAPTER TWENTY-ONE
GAMWELL REVELATIONS

All the speeches and pamphlets, all the handshakes and back slaps, all the meetings and conferences led to one day - Tuesday November 8, 1932, election day. And in a few short hours, it was over. It had been a day of frenzy. Bob's followers had gone nose to nose with Sheriff Blue's bullies and had kept the election honest in Gamwell County.

Everywhere, incumbents were out. Even Philip LaFollette went down to defeat in his bid for another term as governor in Wisconsin. In Gamwell County, Cal Little and Dick Legh were elected by a landslide. Reformers rejoiced.

Marian reflected on the events of the past day while she walked toward the Palace Restaurant. She couldn't describe the exhilaration she felt. Being an integral part of the process that carried them to victory was worth all the toil and fatigue. Marian had a good morning for each person she passed.

Ed Pahnke

They smiled and nodded to each other when they passed, and unlike the previous morning when Marian trudged along shadowy streets, sun shown in a blue sky. Wearing a long black woolen coat, Marian took little notice of the cold. She pressed the fox collar close around her face, and delighted in rubbing her cheeks in the fur.

Arriving in front of the restaurant, she was dazzled by sunlight reflecting on the windows. She entered and found a scattering of people munching their breakfasts. They all seemed relaxed.

Dick Legh and Calvin Little sat in a booth with a bench around three sides of the table. Marian walked directly to the winners, shook their hands, and sat down next to Cal. They wouldn't take office until January of 1933, but the defeated office holders would not dare to take any liberties before then.

Dick reached out and patted her hand. "We heard how you handled that bruiser, Miss Marian. We're proud of you, but I confess I was concerned about your well being."

"Thanks, Dick. I had no intention of letting you and Bob down. I'm certain Bob will want to hear the good news, and I can think of nobody who would more enjoy telling him than I, but there's a problem. I don't know how to find him."

"I'll draw a map for you, Miss Marian," Cal said. He looked out of the high-backed wooden booth to be certain that the walls had no ears or eyes. Assured that nobody was eavesdropping, he resumed his seat in the booth, but before he could start, he saw Reverend Mike Rood striding toward them.

Cups, plates, and silverware were shuffled left to make room in front of Mike. The wooden bench creaked as he eased himself next to Marian.

"Congratulations, Dick, Cal," Mike said.

He shook their hands as each man rose to accept Mike's clasp. He said, "You two are probably eager to start work now instead of waiting until next year."

"Our main concern is to keep Blue and Quennel from enriching themselves before we can provide for the common good," Cal said.

"Well said. Was that from one of your speeches, Cal?" Marian smiled. After the long hours working together during the campaign, she knew Cal well enough to tease him.

"As a matter of fact, it was in one of Blue's speeches. I changed the names, of course. I thought it'd be better for me."

The quartet picked up their coffee cups and clinked them together. "Here, here."

"Now that we've come this far," Dick said, "let's press for disclosure of the evidence against Bob. However, we must not let our friendship for him be known. Otherwise, we could be criticized for prejudice in this case. As it is, should it come to that, I'll have someone else handle his case when it comes to trial."

The hope that lived in Marian's heart lit up her face. "I'm sure Bob would like to know how we're progressing. I'll travel to see him, if someone…" She paused and stared into Cal Little's eyes. His face reddened. She continued, "If someone will give me directions I can follow to reach his hideout, I'll be most appreciative."

After weeks of campaigning, she desperately wanted the election to make a difference for Bob and for the people of the county.

"Here's a rough map of Gamwell County, Miss Marian," Cal said."

He explained the lines and arrows he'd jotted down on the brown paper. Upon seeing the map, she thought runes would have made more sense; but after a bit of coaching, she understood the symbols. She smiled. Now she could get on Traveller any time she wanted and canter off to see Bob. Nobody would know she wasn't off on anything more than a horseback ride.

"I suppose you'd like to start as soon as possible, Miss Marian?" Mike said.

Marian sat scrunched between Reverend Mike and Cal. Their broad shoulders bulged over her slim shoulders squeezing her arms against her bosom and trapping her hands in front of her on the table. She drummed her fingers on the red and white checked oilcloth. "Yes, of course, but I'll be trapped behind a counter at Warton's until Sunday. Speaking of trapped, I'd also appreciate taking full breaths again. Between you and Cal, I feel protected and stifled at the same time."

Mike graciously stood. A pear shaped matron, who happened to be in the aisle, side stepped him to avoid being bowled over. Mike apologized, but she motioned him away. With her nose tilted upward, she continued toward the exit.

Marian edged between Mike and the booth. "I have to go to work now, but I'm certain I'll have as difficult a time waiting for Sunday as a child has waiting for Christmas."

Having finished snipping a piece of flannel yard goods, Marian folded the red and brown material. Opposite her at the counter, Celeste King smiled.

"This will make a fine shirt for Richard, when he returns," Celeste said, lips quivering.

The question of whether Richard King was alive or dead ran through most people's minds. Marian would have rushed to her and embraced her, but being a clerk, she knew she couldn't.

"I suppose you miss teaching," Celeste said, changing the subject. "You were highly regarded."

"Thank you, Mrs. King. I love to teach. Here's your sales slip. Are you finished, or will you be browsing about the store some more?" Marian said wrapping the material in brown paper before handing it to Celeste.

"I'll shop around for a while."

Before they could say good bye, Roland Blue barged up to the counter. He whisked his tan hat off his head and nodded to Mrs. King. She withdrew a few steps to a counter packed with buttons.

"I'm still sheriff, and I'm not stupid." He scowled at Marian. Before she could say a word, he continued, "I see groups of people wearing Filson Cruisers wherever there's trouble or a threat of trouble. They disrupted the arrest at the bank. They showed up at the polls yesterday."

Narrowing his eyes, he stared at Marian. "I even saw you wearing a green coat. I figure people wearing the coats are working with Bob Brunet. What do you think, Miss Marian?"

She felt her face redden. Could she deny the truth?

"I'm certain you saw what you say you saw, Sheriff. However, I wear the coat because it turns away sharp winds. I got my coat through a distress sale at the railroad."

"What do you take me for? If I started wearing a forest-green Filson Cruiser, do you think I'd find things out that would lead to the arrest of Brunet?"

Roland Blue grasped the counter with his hands and smiled. It wasn't the type of smile reserved for babies and puppies.

"I want you to know I'll be watching you, and one day you'll lead me to Brunet. Then I'll pounce."

He lunged toward Marian, and she flinched.

"You don't frighten me, Mister Blue." Still, she knew she had fears, more so than ever. What if she led a stealthy Roland Blue to Bob's hideout? "You'll soon be selling apples because nobody in Gamwell County will employ you."

"I'm not worried. Until I pass the reigns of office to Little, I'll make every effort to capture your Mr. Brunet. Don't take my words lightly." He turned on his heel and left.

Marian swung into the saddle. Mounted on Traveller, she loped off toward the Manitou Hills. She didn't have to refer to the map. It was secured in her jacket pocket, but she had read it so often that she knew the route by memory. The map being close by gave her an extra sense of confidence.

Northern Knights

While she rode, she cast glances in all directions, looking for any sign of being followed. When she reached the one road through the Manitou Hills, she had satisfied herself she was alone, and she continued her ride to see Bob.

She and Traveller became the center of attention when they arrived in the glade. Traveller seemed to like the attention and pranced about en route to the cabin where Marian dismounted into Bob's arms. Marian delighted in having his arms around her, and pulled her face up to Bob's, pressing her lips to his. The cheers of his followers didn't distract her from holding the kiss a full minute.

They waved at the work hardened assemblage before entering the log cabin.

"What's happening beyond the forest, Marian? I'm happy and surprised to see you - on Traveller, no less. What day is it?" He looked at a 1928 calendar nailed to the wall. Without waiting for an answer, he continued, "It feels like Sunday."

"You're right," she said. "I'm here after a successful election in which the powerful fell with a thud. Cal and Dick were elected. After the new-year comes around, you're assured of having a fair hearing. In the next few months, Sheriff Blue will be under close watch."

After a thump on the door, Nat Mutch entered. "Miss Marian, Bob, I'm sorry to bother you, but all of us are curious about the election. When will our lands be returned?"

"We won the election," Marian said. "However, we can't assure anyone the return of his property. I am sorry I can't give you a rousing yes."

"Thank you," Nat said, frowning, and he quickly withdrew.

"Damn," Bob said. "There are no answers to the mysteries surrounding us. Two murders have been committed in the county since I've taken to the woods, and I'm blamed for both. Quennel is still the most powerful man in the county, and I'm a thief in a great forest prison, a king of vagabonds. I've got evidence of wrongdoing, but I don't know what it means."

Marian told him of her findings. "Maybe, just maybe, if you tell me what evidence you have, I'll be able to help you solve some of the mysteries."

She didn't appreciate the look Bob gave her. It seemed to say how could she be of help when he couldn't make sense of the matter? Marian resented the look for a quick moment and then lightened her approach.

"By the look on your face, you're eager for my help. Shoot."

Another expression replaced the haughty look on Bob's face, one of wonder.

The effect Marian desired was accomplished. Everyone who knew her knew she would never use a word such as "shoot" to mean begin.

Bob told of his findings at the bank and at the scene of Joe Worman's murder. When he'd finished, he stared at Marian.

A smile flickered across her face. "Someone who knew of your involvement with the two guns killed both Joe and Clorinda. It's too much of a coincidence to have chosen the revolver you examined and have it turn up as the weapon used to kill Clorinda. As to who it was, I don't know, yet.

"I do know that Elliot Bevis is an executive with District Power. Father has stock in the power company, and I see the name Elliot Bevis in reports. It might be John King and Gil Quennel were paying him off for something, perhaps building a power dam on the Moose Ear River?"

"That's it," Bob said. "What a woman." He hugged her. "Quennel sells the land back to the power company at a profit, and he and John King make a bundle. And he called me a thief? There's one way to find out. I'll confront him, and I'll wring the truth out of him. Damn. That won't work. He'd never admit he's guilty, but if we could find something like a bill of sale for those cattle he claims I stole, that would cinch it."

"If you can get him out of his house or divert his attention, I'll search his office," Marian said.

"Too dangerous," Bob said.

"It won't be dangerous if you can keep him away for thirty minutes. You owe me a chance to prove my worth to you."

Bob thought for a long moment, rubbing his hand across his mouth. Finally, he said, "A kiss will seal the bargain."

He took her in his arms, pressing her to his chest and they kissed.

"I'll alert a couple of the men to back us up, and then it's off to slay the dragon. I haven't seen old Quennel in a couple of months, and I've been itching to take a good whack at him."

CHAPTER TWENTY-TWO
QUENNEL'S CHOICE

Bob and Marian had climbed to the crest of a rocky knoll overlooking the out buildings and chateau belonging to Gil Quennel. Bob wanted to confront Quennel alone, so Will, Nat, and Leo marked time in a camp two miles deep in the forest.

"I'm not so sure that you ought to take the chance of searching Quennel's house," Bob said softly, turning to Marian.

He had been hinting at his uncertainty since they began their hike from his camp. He squirmed to gain a comfortable seat. A wool scarf and bullets for his pistol in the rear-carrying pocket of his coat seemed to shift about with intent to do discomfort. His pistol was in the inside pocket of his coat.

"A fine time to bring this up again," Marian said in a peeved whisper.

Bob looked heavenward in consternation because Marian didn't understand that her well being was his principal concern. The gray and cold sky looked as though it might open any minute to release a flurry of snow.

"Turning your eyes upward won't save your from my wrath."

Bob and Marian spoke in hushed tones, but puffs of steam accentuated their words like tiny smoke signals. Dressed in their woolen Cruisers, their coat collars fended off the biting wind. Woolen caps covered their heads.

Bob's face flushed at her words. "Don't get caught. You know better than I do how he treated you in your own home. There, you successfully fought off his advances. On his own ground, he could prove to be more physical, or he may have you arrested. This is a dangerous stunt, even for a man."

"I'm certain I can be as sneaky as any man can. You know I've been in his home with my father. The household help should be having their dinners around noon, and it's almost twelve o'clock now. I know my way around, and if something is to be found, I'll find it. Do your part and keep him busy. I don't intend to come back empty handed."

She chucked Bob under his chin, hard, and her eyes bored into his.

Bob couldn't understand why she was angry. His motive was to protect her. Were she near the exploding point, she would have turned red - a color in which he did not like her. Such tiffs brought out Marian's free spirit. The first time her temper flared, he was shocked. He ran for verbal cover, but since that first quarrel, he had learned his best bet was to speak calmly.

"Rather than warn me about consequences, we could be half way to Gil's house."

"We'll meet back here," Bob said, sweeping his hand around. The top of the knoll was windswept and barren except for the grove of gray-green spruces that protected Bob and Marian from the northwest wind. The naked branches and twigs of a few scraggly hardwoods scratched and clawed at winter.

Below, surrounded by park-like land, the chateau covered about a quarter acre of ground. It consisted of a fieldstone first floor with logs rising yet another story. The roof peaked in the center, and stone towers stood guard at each corner of the building. A tree lined avenue led to the rambling building.

Ready to go, they both stood, but first, he grabbed her and kissed her with a resounding smack. "For luck," he said.

Eyes closed and a smile on her face, she whispered, "That buss awakened the owls from their slumber."

Bob didn't wait for Marian to open her eyes. He stampeded down the knoll. Arms outstretched, he was half way to the notch, and picking up speed, but his speed threatened to take him up another hill once he reached the valley floor. To brake himself, he dove into a pile of brown leaves and skidded to a halt in the thicket. He jumped to his feet, unhurt. A broad smile on his face, he wigwagged at Marian.

Less flare in her decent, Marian picked her way down the knoll. They trudged along on the valley floor, hand in hand, until they arrived at the avenue that led to the Quennel Chateau.

Bob took to the center of the road. He marched toward Quennel's house in plain sight, and she kept pace dodging from tree to tree. He watched her out of the corner of his eye. Dressed as she was, she blended into the environment, a sort of tumbleweed of the North Country.

Bob boldly walked up the stone steps to the portal, while Marian scampered to the side of the building. Once there, she edged toward a set of French doors that overlooked the parkland.

He grabbed the cast iron knocker. Shaped like an oak leaf, it reminded him of the family crest sewn on some of Quennel's coats. Bob bounced the knocker three times on the ancient wooden door. Some folks said the set of doors was brought from France by Gil Quennel's grandparents and added to the chateau before the turn of the century.

When the door finally opened, it was Byron, Quennel's right hand man who stood in front of Bob. Tottering with age, he rasped, "We accept deliveries in the kitchen." He squinted at Bob as though to recognize him.

"I think Mr. Quennel would wish to talk with me personally." Over Byron's shoulder, he saw Marian glide down a mahogany-paneled hallway toward the rear of the house. "My name is Bob Brunet."

Byron drew in his breath, a look of fear shadowing his face. However, his voice retained a raspy calm. "I will announce you to Mr. Quennel. Please come inside out of the cold."

Bob stepped inside, and Byron pushed the door shut. He shuffled toward a broad staircase. With agonizing slowness, he ascended the steps. Bob paced while waiting. He had counted to two hundred when Quennel appeared. Dressed in a red and black woolen shirt and gray trousers, he descended the stairs quickly using the banister to help him. At the bottom of the steps, he used his cane to walk swiftly and boldly to where Bob stood with his hand extended.

Quennel did not extend his hand for even a perfunctory handshake. "Come to snivel, have you, Brunet?"

Bob reddened, and he clenched his fists.

Quennel tightened his grip on his blackthorn cane and swung it in front of him.

Bob cleared his throat. "More likely you'll be sniveling when I've had my say. I haven't been hiding in a cave since you accused me of theft."

"I dare say not. You've been murdering people at a fast pace."

Bob controlled his anger and concentrated on the speech he had planned, he said, "I have neither murdered nor stolen, as you should know, but I found out why you falsely accused me of theft." Bluffing, he continued, "You wanted to get hold of my property because it has good frontage on the Moose Ear River. You and your cohorts paid off Elliot Bevis of District Power. It was from him that you learned about the proposed land purchases by the District Power. You already have much of the land along the river, and you'll be able to sell it at a handsome, illicit profit soon, or I miss my guess.

"I'm not guessing about the reason for the foreclosures. I obtained proof from King Bank records, and the records will be turned over to the new sheriff. He'll act. All of your riches won't help you then."

The smile had disappeared from Quennel's lips, and he glared at Bob, livid with hate. He crashed his cane against a wooden coat tree and splintered it.

"You have nothing, but I have a taste for your blood. Ever since I first laid eyes on you, you've opposed me," Quennel said. "Now, I want you dead."

When Bob saw Quennel's anger mount, he felt good. He had to snipe at him. "The people in hell want ice water, but they don't get it."

"So you think you will be able leave my home on your own two feet. I have news for you. You won't live to see another sunrise."

"I thought you'd want to fight. I came to talk, but I came prepared to answer your threats, too."

Bob withdrew his twenty-two-caliber pistol from his inside coat pocket.

Showing no fear, Quennel said, "What fight is it if you shoot me. I'm unarmed. We fight this out, man to man. I have sabers. Do you dare fence with me?"

In answer, Bob shed his coat. He slid the pistol into the inside pocket. He had done some fencing in college, and knew that speed and agility were essential to any success. He was faster afoot than Quennel with his game leg, but Bob's college contact with the sport was with foil fencing. In this encounter, he would have to guard against point as well as edge.

The arena in which the fight would take place was about thirty feet square. Along the walls, rough-hewn posts supported a balcony. The great hall was furnished with nothing but a few leather chairs and sofas.

His voice haughty, Quennel said, "Don't worry about bleeding all over the room, Brunet. I'll personally clean up."

Crossed sabers hung below a painting of Gil Quennel's father, Claude. Both father and son had the same gaunt features, hollow eyes, and arrogant smile. Quennel stepped up onto the hearth to remove the sabers from above the stone fireplace. He strode back and offered Bob choice of blades. A bit nervous, Bob took one at random.

The instant Bob had a grip on the hilt of the saber, Quennel cried, "On guard."

After a series of thrusts, parries, and ripostes. Bob knew his speed wouldn't carry him through. Quennel had the fluid motions of one at ease with the saber. His slow footwork was more than compensated for by agile hand movements. Bob was forever on the run, using furniture for allies or closing in to prevent the free use of Quennel's weapon. On such occasions, Quennel used his blackthorn cane to shove or beat Bob back. When Bob jumped back, Quennel lunged after him with a mocking laugh.

In attempts to take him off guard, Bob would scamper backward quickly. At such times Quennel would burst out with the old axiom, "You can run but you can't hide." Bob gnashed his teeth together but kept dodging around chairs and posts. When he felt Quennel would least expect it, he lunged forward in a running attack thrusting his blade forward in a series of small semicircular movements, a sort of poor man's disengage. Quennel parried the attack and launched his own riposte. Bob could not reverse himself quickly enough. Quennel's saber dug into Bob's shoulder. Bob was pinned, his back against one of the posts.

"Good by, Brunet," Quennel said and laughed.

Bob tried to switch his saber from one hand to the other, but Quennel beat the sword out of his hand with a swipe of his blackthorn cane. Withdrawing the blade from Bob's shoulder with a lightening move, Quennel thrust forward with equal speed.

Before the blade struck him, Bob dropped to the floor, and crawled toward his saber. Quennel couldn't stop the force of his thrust. His blade struck the post, bent, and snapped. Meanwhile, Bob, saber in hand, scrambled to his feet, facing Quennel. Even without a saber in his hand, Quennel didn't show fear. Brandishing his cane, he attacked Bob.

"I'll not back down now, Brunet." But Quennel's blackthorn was no match for a saber.

"We dueled with your weapons," Bob said. "Let's try mine, handguns in your forest.

"Do you know the knoll at the end of your lane? I'll be out there waiting, if you're brave enough to face me."

A sneer curled Quennel's lips. "Brave! No man dares call me a coward to my face. The forest it is."

With a mighty heave, Bob launched his saber toward the ceiling. It stuck. After picking up his coat, he strode outdoors - his element - his world.

CHAPTER TWENTY-THREE
FOREST FRACAS

Bob's shoulder throbbed, but he was determined not to let Quennel know how badly injured he was. A weapon other than his twenty-two-caliber pistol would be difficult to handle. With measured steps, he beat back the rubber in his knees. He breathed deeply, and the cold air revived him. He began to plan for the fight Quennel would bring to him. In close Bob would have a good chance. He passed another tree, a milepost of sorts on his route to the valley. He turned up his collar. The dampness of his blood felt cold on his arm. Another tree. Soon he'd be able to rest for a bit.

He lifted the flap on his coat pocket with his left hand and eased his hand inside to touch the gold wedding band. What he was trying to accomplish had meaning. His striving got him a little closer to Marian, to victory.

A snowflake landed on his nose. The road that led away from Quennel's chateau was shielded from the elements by the line of trees, and he hadn't noticed the dusting of snow on the surrounding parkland. This could be another factor in his favor. Another tree. Pass two more and he'd be swallowed up by the valley. He plodded forward.

Once in the valley, he could quickly care for his shoulder. After that he'd wait for Quennel in the grove of spruces on the knoll.

First he had to rest, for a moment. With the choice between the ground and a boulder, he slumped down onto the boulder, muscles relaxed. He had to prepare himself mentally for Quennel, and the most comfortable chair in his home could serve him no better. He regained his composure.

Unbuttoning his coat, he withdrew his pistol from the inside pocket of his coat. He made certain the clip was full. He had put ten bullets in the clip, but he checked again. His shoulder throbbed. He placed the pistol on the boulder next to him. With his left hand, he unfastened the flap on the rear-carrying pocket and dug around until he got hold of the box of cartridges. Ten shots should be enough, but having more ammunition wouldn't hurt. He slipped off the right sleeve of his coat before removing a wool scarf from the carrying pocket. He replaced the box of bullets in the pocket and buttoned it.

He wound, then tied the tan scarf around his wound. Though bulky, the bandage would have to do. He struggled to get his right arm back through the sleeve and button his coat to the collar.

Snow had begun to cover the ground, and when he stood, he brushed off flakes that had accumulated on his shoulders. It was time to go. Setting his face into the breeze, he began the trek up the knoll to the place he'd picked, to fight Quennel.

The grove of spruces stood against the wind and the snow. Snow swirled thickly about by the time he arrived in their shelter, and he had to squint to see even the edge of the knoll. He sat behind a fallen tree out of the snow, planning. He'd face Quennel when he got close enough for an unobstructed shot. Bob had won numerous shooting matches, and was considered the best shot in the county, or state for that matter. Shooting out the eye of a turkey at twenty yards proved his reputation. A weak smile lit his wind burned face.

Quennel could appear out of a squall at any time. To be prepared, Bob unbuttoned his coat to draw his pistol.

He dug his hand deeply into an empty pocket. He had plenty of bullets, but where was the pistol. Throwing bullets at Quennel seemed futile.

"Where the hell?" He said. As though looking for a grain of sand, he continued to feel around in the pocket. He groaned. "Damn it. It's gone."

He searched his memory as thoroughly as he had searched his pocket. The boulder! He had put it on the boulder when he was resting, but he had looked around before starting up the knoll. Had it slipped down next to the boulder? There was no choice. A gunfight with no gun was a joke, a joke with a deadly punch line. He had to go back, but backtracking could confront him with Quennel. The pistol had to be by the boulder, unless Quennel had found it.

After buttoning his coat, he circled on the opposite side of the knoll, the side toward the chateau. Grabbing hands full of brush and using entrenched rocks to prevent himself from sliding, he threaded his way back down the steep side toward the bottom. His wound stiffened his right shoulder. He swung his arm to keep it loose, though he knew he should keep his arm still to keep from agitating the wound. He used his left arm to support and steady himself.

A misstep would send him down into a tangle of brush where Quennel might be waiting to pick him off after the noise had subsided. Wind sprayed snow into his face. He squinted to see footholds. Rest was out of the question though his left hand was numbed from the icy rocks and limbs. He had rubbed a hole through his canvas mitten. Red, callused, his palm showed through.

Was there no bottom to the knoll? The west side had to be a greater height than the east. He sat on his buttocks and slid the last few feet to level ground.

The circuitous route had finally landed him in the notch. Each step he took, he looked for signs of Quennel, but he saw no tracks. When the boulder came into view, Bob picked up his pace. Before reaching it, he sighted a second set of tracks in the snow, heading up the hill.

Upon reaching the boulder, Bob trembled, not from cold, but from trepidation. An awful dread filled his mind while he scratched through the snow and leaves around the pink quartzite boulder. His worst fears vanished when his hand touched the barrel of his pistol. The bore of the twenty-two-caliber semiautomatic looked free of clogged snow. Brushing the snow from the gun, he prayed it would fire when he pulled the trigger.

The only way to find out was to fire it at Quennel. To that end, he followed Quennel's tracks. Snow had not yet filled them in, and his quarry might be just seconds ahead.

Bob's head throbbed as much as his shoulder. There would be no time for buck fever when he and Quennel sighted each other, but Bob had never shot at a man before. He breathed deeply to calm himself.

Pistol in hand, he climbed toward the crest of the hill.

"Hello, Brunet." It was Gil Quennel's voice.

Bob looked up. Quennel stood not twenty feet away, the muzzle of a revolver pointed at him.

"I wanted you to see it coming, Brunet."

Bob dropped to the ground. He slid back.

Quennel fired. Both hands in front of him, Bob flipped off the safety and steadied his gun. Quennel was in his sights. He fired. Once. Twice.

Quennel tumbled backward. Bob scrambled to his feet. A slipping and sliding dash brought him up the knoll to Quennel's side. He dropped to his knees.

"You win, Brunet. They said you were the best shot in the county. I'll vouch for it in heaven, or hell. I lied about the theft." He coughed. "I beat everyone but you, the one I wanted most to beat…"

Until the last word, Bob didn't notice a pair of black boots and olive trousers hovering over him.

"On your feet," Sheriff Roland Blue commanded. "You're under arrest for murder, two of them."

"How the hell did you get here so fast?"

Blue's reply was terse, "Quennel's man, Byron, called me. I heard shots."

"I'm not goin' to jail for something I didn't do."

He slammed his pistol to the ground, scrambled to his feet, and began to bob and weave. Blue holstered his forty-five, balled his hands into fists, and stalked after Bob. Bob threw a left hook that landed on Blue's chest. Blue crossed a right that connected on Bob's chin. He staggered. His shoulder no longer ached. He lurched forward, arms flailing. A huge fist whistled toward him.

He saw it but couldn't avoid it. When it struck, night closed in on him.

CHAPTER TWENTY-FOUR
THOSE JAILHOUSE BLUES

"Wake up, Bob," a voice called out of the blackness. How could a sunny spring day be so cold? "Wake up," the voice called again.

Coming from a warm dream into cold pain was no bargain. Bob opened his eyes. "Marian? Did you hit me?"

She knelt next to Bob gazing at him.

"I did," Blue said. "Get up. You're goin' to jail." His voice sounded colder than any winter day.

Bob stared at his wrists. Handcuffs shackled them.

"It seems all I can hold you for you for is the murder of Joe Worman, and maybe Clorinda Vinette. Murder is enough." A wicked smile crossed his lips and his eyes narrowed. "Miss Marian explained the rest away."

Bob looked fondly at Marian. They were a good team. Breaking up was hard to do. That sounded like a good song title. Maybe someone would write it, some day.

"Anyhow, I heard Mr. Quennel confess the frame. Too bad you couldn't wait to get even with Joe."

"I didn't kill him. I found him dead. Then I was conked on the head."

He dragged himself to his feet with Marian's help. She threw her arms around him and showered him with kisses. Her cool lips pressed against his flushed face. He hadn't realized his face felt so hot. His lips burned. Was he feverish from the wound? What did it matter? He longed to tear the handcuffs to shreds and bury Marian in his arms.

"Move along," Blue said.

Prodded by the lawman, he dragged his feet toward the automobile waiting below. Walking drained him, but before reaching the edge of the hill, he looked back. Marian blew him a kiss and forced a weak smile.

Bob half skidded, half-stumbled down the knoll. Once in the valley, he felt weak while he plodded toward the lane where Blue had parked his Model A.

With each step, he tottered. Blue grabbed his arm and jacked him up. Bob looked down to assure himself his feet were moving. They barely scraped the snow. When Bob and the sheriff finally reached the automobile, it was nothing but a blur to Bob. Blue propped him up against it before pushing him inside. After tumbling onto the back seat, he remembered nothing until he woke up in a warm jail cell.

His arm was bandaged, and he was dressed in clean clothes.

He struggled to his feet and, a little wobbly at first, waited until he felt stronger. He concentrated on walking toward the mirror that hung on the gray brick wall. When he looked into the stainless steel mirror, a jailbird with thick stubble on his face stared back. He scraped his hand across his beard before turning. Three steps brought him to the bars of his cell door. Like a caged wild animal, he rattled the barred door.

Heavy steps clicked on the concrete floor, and Bob craned his neck to see who was coming. Deputy Howard Thorne appeared. Stopping in front of Bob, he grinned at the prisoner.

"May I have some food?" Bob asked. "I've an awful gnawing in my stomach."

"Supper's at five," Howard said. He wiped a film of grease from his lips, his jowls shaking when he spoke.

"How about a razor and lather to shave myself?"

"Sheriff Blue's cousin will be in to shave you tomorrow. Sheriff ain't taking no chances with you getting anything sharp." He sucked his teeth. "Anything else?"

"When can I have visitors?" He felt like he was begging. Would he learn to shuffle like a chain gang prisoner? At that moment he vowed to escape.

"Miss Marian left word to be told when you woke up. What she sees in a devil like you when there's honest men about, I'll never know. She'll be here tomorrow about eight in the morning."

Marian paid Bob many visits over the next month. Christmas was about to come, but nothing in Bob's cell marked the holiday. Home-cooked meals and no exercise put weight on Bob's lean frame. He'd stare out his window into the wood lot beyond the fence. He spied a deer running free. Black-capped chickadees perched on his windowsill for a moment before flying off in their perpetual search for food. Each wild thing he saw put a deeper longing in his heart to be free.

A trial date had been set for late January, with bail having been denied. He wouldn't have given a plugged nickel for his chances.

An ever-widening gloom settled over him, but Marian's visits helped him maintain a semblance of hope. Sheriff Blue continued to snub Bob, or so he thought. The sheriff had not looked in on him for several days.

"Miss Marian's here, Bob," Howard Thorne said. He plunked a chair down in front of the cell door.

Dressed in her full length, black wool coat with a fox collar, Marian hurried along the corridor in high leather boots. December winds had colored her cheeks to match the sprig of holly berries fastened to her coat. There was no doubt, she was happy. Her whole demeanor reflected it.

"Good morning, Bob. Good news for Alice and Reverend Mike."

"What happened?"

She looked at Howard. He seemed about to speak. "No fair telling, Mr. Thorne. I'm the official bearer of good news in this jail."

"I ain't saying a word."

He shuffled back toward the outer office.

Marian glanced furtively about as though to assure herself that she and Bob were alone, and she laughed nervously. Her hand shook when she passed a slip of paper to Bob and motioned him to hide it.

Nonchalantly, he stuck his hand in the pocket of his wool plaid shirt. Before remembering that all of his personal articles had been impounded, he felt for the gold wedding band. The pocket was empty. His heart stopped. Then he remembered, and quickly buttoned the pocket containing the note.

"Are you well, Bob?" she asked. Her lips remained parted as though to be ready respond.

"Oh, as well as can be expected. I thought I lost something. Sometimes, I forget I'm in jail. Looking outside makes me feel even worse when I'm locked up inside. I've been snowbound in a lean-to, but nothing matches this helpless feeling. Outside I can try to prove myself innocent."

Each time Marian visited him. Bob grew a little more disconsolate. The smell of her perfume lingered in the cellblock after she left. At times like that, he didn't know whether he wanted her back or wished she had never visited him.

Seeming to disregard his complaints, she asked, "Now do you want to hear the good news?"

"Of course," he said. Then in a whisper, he asked, "When do I read?"

"Later. I'll tell the story from the beginning.

"Reverend Mike and Sheriff Blue were at a Community Club meeting, but they avoided each other. As the evening wore on, Roland Blue became more boisterous. I suspect he had a bottle of liquor. He bragged about his manhood and belittled Reverend Mike.

"Finally, he swaggered, staggered would probably be closer to it, to where Reverend Mike was chatting with friends. He got Reverend Mike's attention, looked him in the eye and said, 'If you and my daughter make fancy together, I'll pulverize you. You know God damn well I can do it.'

"I'm quoting now. Don't think those are my words. Cal Little even blushed when he told me the story.

Bob smiled because he understood Marian and loved her.

"Reverend Mike stood and said, 'What you say about Alice in public is better left unsaid. Better yet, such things shouldn't even be thought of. And she is your daughter.'

"Sheriff Blue grabbed Reverend Mike by his coat lapels and tried to yank him, but Mike didn't budge. He said, 'I'm going to teach you a lesson for talking back to me, Bible Boy.'

"He dug a left fist to Reverend Mike's stomach, but Mike didn't wince. Reverend Mike rarely gets angry, but he won't take abuse forever. He jabbed Sheriff Blue once. I'm using Cal's words. The sheriff attempted to connect with a roundhouse right. Using both hands, Reverend Mike threw Sheriff Blue against a wall. Dented it, I understand. Before the sheriff could recover, Reverend Mike slammed a left hook to his head. The sheriff tried to fend Reverend Mike off by pawing at him with left jabs, but Reverend Mike threw a right cross - whatever that is - to the sheriff's head.

"Roland Blue crumpled to the floor.

"When Cal Little doused him with water - with relish Cal claimed - the sheriff woke and said, 'Mike Rood's a man after all.'

"With the help of a chair, Roland Blue stumbled to his feet and said, 'Rood, come back here.'

"Reverend Mike had walked away to regain his composure. He probably thought the sheriff wanted to continue the brawl, but nothing could have been further from the truth.

"Sheriff Blue said, 'So, Son, you and Alice want to get married. A man like you'll make a damn fine son-in-law.'

"They shook hands to seal the agreement. Alice and Reverend Mike are officially engaged."

Marian smiled broadly before continuing, "Cal Little told me the entire story. I would've enjoyed that brawl.

"By all accounts, Sheriff Blue respects only brute force."

Bob smiled. It was the kind of grin people associated with his personality before trouble began to pile on his shoulders. "Blue flattened? That's great. Mike's a mighty man, no denying that. Seeing him lift a mule off the ground on his shoulders, if only for a few seconds, proved that to me. Fighting side by side with him would be an honor."

His smile waned and disappeared, and Bob lapsed back into his melancholy. "Too bad I won't make it to their wedding. Thanks for visiting me, but you'd best get on with your life too, Marian."

"I'm ashamed of you for getting so depressed. Where's the fighter I knew? We're so close to winning. Roadblocks are merely detours that force us to take a little longer to reach our goals."

"You sound like I used to before…"

"I should go now," she said. Was that a tear in her eye?

She pressed her face to the bars. Their lips met. When they kissed, he believed, if only for an instant, that he could possibly prove his innocence, regain his property, and wed Marian. Their lips parted, but Bob still felt the warmth of Marian.

"We may tell our children of the joys of kissing through bars. Don't forget," She shaped the words with her lips. "the note."

Northern Knights

Marian turned and sauntered away. Even wearing a winter coat, she had a natural way of swinging her hips that kept Bob's attention focused on her. Without her steadfast love, confinement would have been unbearable, but he had to face facts. In a county still run by John King, there was no bail, but if there were bail, he didn't have enough money.

After she disappeared through the doorway, his glance went to the clock hanging above the door on the brick wall. He watched the pendulum swinging back and forth. With his mind's eye he saw her. He had never thought as much about Marian as he had since they began working together to solve his problems. With difficulty, he erased her from his thoughts.

Nobody else was in the cellblock, and Bob was certain nobody could see him; however, taking no chances, he slumped down in the farthest corner of the cell to read the note. After unfolding the paper, he began reading. It seemed to Bob that he'd seen the small, well-formed letters somewhere before, but where?

Dear Bob,

The time is right. Be ready tonight to take flight. We will don our green cruisers and be at the jail a eight o'clock, sharp. Try not to be away. We will cause a ruckus to divert attention away from you. Roland Blue will be at supper with Alice and Mike, so we don't have to fear he will bollix up plan.

What I have said so far would not work if Wendell, the janitor, was not in on the escape. We have a key to your cell. No matter how we got it. Suffice to say we toasted Miss Marian's daring.

195

When Wendell comes in to clean up tonight, he will be wearing a blue uniform. If you've noticed, you and he are about the same size. He will start his chores as usual at seven forty-five. When eight o'clock chimes on the clock in your corridor, he will open the cell. At the same time, we will start banging on windows and doors. You two will change. Put on his cap too. Lock him inside after punching his clock. Don't be afraid to start a little blood running.

There's no rear door out of the cellblock. You have to sweep your way out the front door. Pull the cap down over your face. When we see you coming, we'll clear a path.

Wait behind Sawyer's Sawmill. Transportation will be forthcoming.

We are not getting you anything else for Christmas.

Your friends,

All of us.

The word "freedom" slipped from Bob's lips when he finished the note.

Not wanting to take a chance that a deputy would discover it, Bob tore it up and flushed it down the toilet. With the plan firmly set in his mind, he closed his eyes and day dreamed while he waited.

CHAPTER TWENTY-FIVE
THE LITTLE MAN WHO WASN'T THERE

"God rest you merry gentlemen."

Wendell sang while he scrubbed, the smell of Lysol hanging in the air. He had never sung before, but understandably, he felt nervous. Getting jailed, or punched in the nose, or both was not appealing. The minute hand toiled its way up the face of the clock toward twelve. Bob watched it. Wendell watched it.

Howard Thorne walked through the doorway, and looked at Bob and Wendell.

"Folks who watch the clock will always remain one of the hands," he said and laughed.

Bob turned to the gray wall. His palms oozed sweat. Wendell scrubbed the cement floor and sang with renewed vigor. Clearing his throat, Bob added his hoarse voice to the carol. When he looked out from back of the bars, he saw Howard with his hands to his ears. Bob sang louder. Muttering something about cruel and unusual punishment, Howard left.

The minute hand had almost reached its apex when a stir out front developed into a commotion. Wendell leaped to Bob's cell door, key in hand. He fumbled at the lock. "Don't worry. Don't worry," he kept whispering.

The door opened. Wendell entered. Bob sent him sprawling with a left hook.

"You all right?"

Wendell rubbed his jaw. First he shook his head yes, then no. He handed Bob his battered slouch hat before removing his uniform and handing it to Bob. Bob yanked Wendell's clothes over his own.

After locking the cell door, Bob began mopping his way to the office entrance. While swinging the mop, he shook the sting of the punch out of his left hand, and tried to think calmly. What could go wrong? The two deputies, the usual number on duty in the evening, must be entangled in a melee of some kind that Bob's friends had started.

Bob pulled his hat down over his ears before removing the mop from the bucket of water. With a plop, it hit the floor. He swished the mop from side to side, barely wetting the floor while he moved nearer the door. Upon reaching the door to the sheriff's office, he butted it open with the end of his mop.

The door swung open revealing an uproar. Bob smiled, ducked, and plowed ahead. The deputies were enveloped by maybe seven or eight green coated men. Their shoulders and hips kept the deputies busy shifting about while a constant stream of loud questions prevented the deputies from gathering their wits.

Mop splashing water at a brisk pace and head bent, he watched the ruckus from beneath the brim of the hat. Bob's men had maneuvered the deputies away from the railing that separated sheriff's personnel from ordinary citizenry. He recognized the men, but neither Nat, Will, or Leo was there. Nobody seemed to be paying the least attention to him.

Breathing more easily, he was about to drop the mop and grab the doorknob when the door flew open.

Instead of a closed door, he faced a snarling, gun wielding, Roland Blue. He stepped inside, but blocked the door. Then he moved. He didn't seem to recognize Bob. His glance darted around the room. Did he know Bob was loose?

Blue pointed his nickel-plated revolver at the ceiling. Certainly he wouldn't put a hole in the ceiling the way he had done in the church. The gun roared. The roar and a shower of plaster stilled the mob.

"Where the hell is Bob Brunet?" Sheriff Blue shouted.

No answer.

Bob knew his avenue of escape would soon be covered, so he acted quickly.

He pointed the business end of the mop forward and charged at full tilt, slamming the mop into Blue's stomach. Blue grunted and tumbled to the wooden floor.

Sprawled on his side, he gasped, "It's Brunet. Shoot him."

Bob dashed through the front door and continued along Pioneer Street. The temperature hovered around zero. In the cloudless sky, the Northern Lights were on display. A quick look back told him his men had followed his lead.

A glut of green coats spilled into the street. More gun fire. They scattered. Blue plunged through the doorway, and looked left and right. Again, Bob began to run.

"Halt!" Blue shouted.

The word put wings on Bob's feet. Stopping to look for his men may have been a mistake. How did Blue get there anyway?

After three steps, Bob was running. Past snow piles three feet high, past black store windows, past wooden lampposts, he dashed.

The bullet splattered against the wall of the Palace Restaurant. Bob had to turn at the next street. The rear of Sawyer's Sawmill was all he could think of. Inhaling giant gulps of frigid air, he exhaled puffs of steam. Ahead the sign for Grant Avenue clung to a lamppost.

When he reached Grant Avenue, he raced around the corner at a forty-five degree angle, a mistake. He slid into a pile of ice and snow, but he righted himself and pounded ahead. Spread out in front of him was the sawmill. The Radisson River, likely ice covered, flowed in back of the mill.

Heedless of obstacles, he raced past stacks of logs and plank shanties. Would an automobile be waiting for him? When he reached a gravel road, he stopped. A block long, the road fronted the river. He stared along the road, but there was no sign of life. A half dozen black trucks were parked between piles of logs and lumber. Lungs pounding, he began to half run half walk along the road inspecting his surroundings.

"Over here, Bob," someone whispered.

Was that the click from the hammer of a gun being cocked?

He saw nobody.

"By the truck, Bob," the whispering voice said, sounding closer.

Bob pressed forward, trying to see through the gloom. Did he hear the sound of a muffled chuckle? Nobody stepped forward. Why the game of hide-and-seek?

"In back of you, Bob."

Bob Whirled around. Nat Mutch stood there, gun pointed at Bob.

"Nat? Why the games? It's me, Bob."

"I know that damn well. You're an escaped fugitive, and I have every right to shoot you on sight. How did you escape Blue? More of that Brunet luck? Well, you're luck's run out."

"This isn't funny, Nat." Beads of sweat broke out on his forehead.

"There's no joke in my words. Does a prankster like you understand that? You've served your purpose, but there's no time for last wishes."

"Drop that gun you little turn coat."

It was Will's voice. Good old, dour Will.

Nat Mutch spun on his heel. He flicked the trigger of his revolver once, but the bullet missed Will. Will returned the fire with a slug from his twelve gauge. The slug propelled Nat six feet back. He raised his arms to clutch at his chest, then dropped to the road.

Bob and Will rushed to their fallen foe, but the little man was dead.

"You surely saved my butt this time, Will. But why did he want to kill me, and how did you figure it out?"

"No time for talk now. There's a sleigh across the river. That little skunk told us to have a flivver waiting at the Cross Roads General Store. No chance to get there now. You're shaking, pard."

"I've got only these coveralls over my shirt and trousers. Let's get the hell across the river."

Out of the dark came voices. "I heard shots."

"This way."

"Follow me," Will said.

After sliding down the embankment to the river, they made their way to the other side. In places, they skirted slabs of ice wedged over the ice field. They kept low, but the clear night was their enemy, too.

A voice carried in the cold night air. "Somebody's crossing the river."

"After 'em."

Breathless from running, Bob and Will reached the shore and looked back. Black shapes appeared on the ice at the opposite shore.

"There's the sleigh," Will said.

"Let's jingle those bells," Bob said.

They leaped to the seat of the red and green sleigh, and Will flicked the reins once, twice, and a third time to get the horses to a trot. Soon they were out of sight of the river, but the trail left by the sleight runners would be easy to follow.

"I know what you're thinking," Will said. "But once we reach the trunk highway our tracks will be lost with those that have gone before us.

We leave this rig at Zebulon's Inn. He'll stow the sleigh and stable the horses.

"We stay there for the night. In the morning, we can set out for camp."

Ushered into a lantern lit room, Bob began thawing immediately. A potbellied stove glowed in one corner of the room. Two beds, covered with red, green, and yellow crazy quilts thick enough to float on air, beckoned to their tired bodies. Three wooden chairs, a table, and a commode completed the furnishings. A pitcher of water and basin stood on the oak veneer commode.

Bob stood warming his hands over the stove while Will harangued. "I never really trusted Nat. Too many coincidences."

"Lucky for me you had suspicions."

"You're too trusting. Someone's got to take a good hard look at what's going on."

"Now everybody knowing anything about Richard King's kidnapers has ended up dead. I had time in jail to form ideas, but Nat's involvement changes things. Damn! Who are the kidnapers? Their identity's as much a mystery now as it was when Richard was kidnapped in June. What made you suspect Nat?"

"I'd tell you if you'd stop buttin' in." Will glowered. "It wasn't until after a while that I started to put two and two together. First, he suddenly appears when we find the clearing. Next, he knows Clorinda when we first meet her. He says all the forest folk know her. I checked around, but none of the men, except Leo, knew her. Lots of them heard of her though. How could Joe's murderer know you'd be taking Marian to visit Clorinda? Nat must o' helped to set you up for the frame. He was out huntin' most of the time you was away, or so he said. When we planned to set you free, he wrote the note."

"The note," Bob broke in. "I remember where I saw that Palmer Method handwriting before. Nat wrote the first ransom note, but who did he work for?"

Will cleared his throat, "Can I continue?"

"Go ahead."

"He never showed the note to nobody, but Miss Marian saw it. The plan called for all of us to go to the jail, but he said we'd be sure be recognized. At first, I was to wait in camp, and he was going to wait at the Cross Roads General Store with the truck. With all the things that had happened before, I wondered. I said I'd wait at Zebulon's instead of camp. They went on ahead. Young Zeb borrowed me a horse and sleigh, and I followed Nat, but he didn't stay at the Cross Roads General Store.

"When all the fellows left for the jail, Nat drove to Sawyer's. I crossed the river at the bridge, parked the sleigh, and hiked over the ice to the sawmill. I had to go like hell to make it there by eight. I never did see Nat until he stepped out with the gun."

"There has to be something that'll lead us to the kidnapers, Will, something we're missing. Let's sleep on it."

Will extinguished the lamp, and both men fell into the beds. Bob lay in the bed, his eyes wide open, staring at the ceiling. Only the red glow cast by the potbellied stove lighted the room.

The kidnappers had to be the murderers too, but who were they. John King certainly had reason to want his brother out of the way. Were Blue and Quennel involved for the money? It had to be one of them. Will said Bob was too trusting, so he'd try to reason this out without emotion. Who were the suspects? The first suspect was Leo Long Mane, but he was their friend, wasn't he?

Bob continued to stare at the ceiling, thinking.

CHAPTER TWENTY-SIX
WINTER HAUNTS

Snow covered trees encircled the glade. Bob stared through the cabin window at the stark white sentinels against the ice blue sky. Under their ghostly white clothes, they awaited the liberation of spring. They knew nothing of Christmas, which was less than a week away.

During autumn, the men in Bob's tiny settlement had labored collecting provisions for the long winter. They had looked forward to a time of relaxing and feasting. Shut in by snow, they gathered to eat and tell stories. Not so Bob, he was free for a reason. He couldn't afford to allow time to pass because his reputation would be tarnished even more so by his escape, and he didn't want to spend Christmas as a fugitive.

When Bob returned to camp, he had greeted and shook the hand of each of his men. After the back thumping and warm greetings, he'd retired to his cabin to rest. After six weeks in jail his head was packed with ideas. Various theories as to the identity of Joe Worman's and Clorinda Vinette's murderer or murderers and to the whereabouts of Richard King screamed to be tested.

Where to start was the question in his mind. The Church at the Corners? The King Bank? Clorinda's log home? Each place seemed significant. The elusive John King and Sheriff Blue were the remaining scoundrels, but were there others to be searched out? Could Leo be involved somehow? He threw that idea from his mind.

Could Celeste King supply some answers? He knew there was risk, but he resolved to question her.

He had asked himself about the tie between Joe Worman and Nat Mutch, but there seemed to be no answer. Why he had never considered Nat Mutch a suspect worried him, but he had concluded he was too trusting about some people - not Leo though - and put it out of his mind. Why did he suddenly suspect Leo?

Since Bob lived as a fugitive in the Manitou Hills, he decided the best place to begin his investigation was at Clorinda's home. The house was locked in by winter, but he had a feeling something important might be there.

The first day after his return, Bob moped around the cabin. When even the piquant odor of wood smoke sent his thoughts to the forest wilderness, he decided to start his journey the next day and got busy packing.

In a corner of the cabin, he piled heavy wool trousers and a heavy mackinaw-type short coat. He shoved a compass into a mackinaw pocket. His tuque - knitted for him by his mother - would keep his head warm. Wool socks, leather pacs, and clothe mittens filled out his clothing needs. Then he rolled up his rabbit skin blanket. Going after big game demanded a rifle, so he borrowed an old Winchester lever-action .30-30 from Sylvlus, one of his men.

A pair of Chippewa style snowshoes hung from the rafters. Slightly over a foot wide and three and a half feet long, the square-toed snowshoes were made for country such as the Manitou Hills. Bob mounted a chair, cut the snowshoes down, and inspected them. They looked sound.

Since he planned to be away for only a day and return the next, he didn't have to pack much food.

When Will asked why he was packing. Bob said, "I'm arranging my gear."

One day of rest after his escape was enough. If he wasn't doing something, he'd feel as though he were back in a cell. He had to talk with Will before he ventured into the northern bush alone, but he intended to wait until early morning to explain. They shared the cabin while the other men were scattered throughout the glade in sundry shelters. There was also one large lodge for meetings.

After a silent supper, Bob stood up. "I'm going outside for a while."

He wound a wool muffler around his neck and snugged a red cap over his ears. Will continued to shovel bread and venison into his mouth. "Don't let the cold in when you leave."

Bob buttoned the last button on his black and blue mackinaw while standing at the door. When he opened the door, a wall of cold smacked him in the face. He turned up his collar and stepped outside.

Smoke rose straight up from a half dozen chimneys. Bob looked up into the night sky. A curtain of northern lights veiled millions of stars in the clear sky. Reds, greens, and yellow-greens waxed and waned above him. A milky red would gather overhead, drift away, only to be replaced with green. A gauzy red would slowly mask the green.

His attention fastened on nature's show, Bob's mind wandered. He remembered Christmas when he was a boy. His father had cut a balsam fir from the forest. A rainbow of fragile glass ornaments had hung on the tree. Candles perched on the branches amid circles of melted wax. A fire glowed in the fireplace, where stockings had hung to wait for Saint Nicholas. The smell of sugar cookies, apple pies, mince pies, and golden pound cake had mingled and teased his senses until his mouth watered.

His memories drifted away, like the vivid red from the northern lights melting into eternity. In his mind, the log lodge he called home glowed with the lights and love of Christmas. The vision grew even more faint. If he were prevented from returning, would the memory eventually disappear?

He stamped his feet before beginning to trudge around the glade. When he neared the huge bull spruce that dominated the glade, a shadow flitted across his face. Looking up, Bob saw a great horned owl glide silently past. Like that shadow, Bob had touched and turned many lives. Now he had to turn his own life around.

With each step, he became more certain that he must return to Clorinda Vinette's house to begin to solve the mystery.

At six the next morning, he tried to rouse Will, but the man was a log under his olive drab blanket. To awaken him, Bob turned him on to his back and tickled his ribs. Will guffawed, slapped at Bob, and blinked his eyes open.

"Are my presents under the tree? Oh, Bob. I was dreaming… What the hell's wrong?"

"Nothing's wrong. I'm going on an expedition looking for a raindrop in a river—alone. I got my gear together yesterday."

"What the hell you talkin' about, Bob? You won't find water nowhere, accept by some spring hole."

Bob smiled. Will didn't remember saying that it would be as likely finding a raindrop in a river as finding Richard King. He hoped to prove Will wrong.

Instead of explaining further, he said, "I'm going hunting."

He didn't mention that he planned to hunt for game more dangerous and illusive than any other that roved the northern bush. The kidnappers were his quarry, but before telling anybody else his theory, he had to convince himself that he was on the right road. Questions from anyone en route to discovery, even Will, would make him nervous. No matter, he could take care of himself. He had proved himself in his encounter with Quennel, but that time he was armed with some proof of Quennel's guilt. Questions replaced proof on this expedition.

"You woke me up to tell me I can go back to sleep? Damn it, Bob, if I knew you was going to be such a pest, I'd've left you turn gray in jail." He pulled the covers back over him.

"I don't want anyone wondering about me and following me. That's why I'm letting you know I'll return tomorrow."

Suddenly, Will sat up in bed. Wrinkling his nose, he said, "Do I smell coffee and griddlecakes?"

"Your nose and your stomach must have a direct link. By the way, would you like pancakes for breakfast?"

At the invitation for food, Will threw the covers off the bed and jumped to his feet. Don't mind if I do," he said. Not bothering to don his trousers, he wore red flannels and gray wool socks when he scuffed to the kerosene stove.

When they first occupied the cabin, the stove was in a sad state of disrepair. A relic of past residents, it had gathered a coat of rust and dust, but Bob had cleaned it and repaired it.

"I take back what I said. I'll miss your cooking when you're gone. You put an Indian guide to shame."

It was not faint praise when Will complimented a person. He armed himself with a knife and fork and sat behind his plate waiting to be served.

"I may cook like a guide, but I don't wait on people. Bring your plate. I'll throw on the cakes."

Bob tucked away ten pancakes and a half-pound of bacon. He would need the fat to ward off the cold. Whenever Will asked a question, Bob pointed to his mouth full of food, and said nothing.

Before tramping off into the snowy wilderness on his snowshoes, Bob shook Will's sticky hand. Will's attempts to wipe the maple syrup off on the front of his union suit had been unsuccessful. When Bob opened the door, his hand stuck to the doorknob for an instant. A blast of cold air blew inside. With the door open, the two sidekicks said good-by.

"Damn, it's cold out there," Will said. "Let's keep our talking brief. I think my marrow's freezing up."

Bob thumped Will on his back and slyly rubbed his syrupy hand on his back. Then he plunged into the white wilderness.

CHAPTER TWENTY-SEVEN
A COLD RECEPTION

Bob had almost forgotten why he made the trek across the white wilderness. His spirits were lifted by the freedom he felt, and his senses focused on beauty nature sculpted out of snow. The ache in his legs caused by trudging through the trackless snow disappeared after a few miles, and his snowshoes seemed to float over the snow.

Winter had altered the landscape, and Bob referred to his compass often to confirm his route.

Hours passed before he reached the main road through the Manitou Hills wilderness. Horses and cutters had trampled the snow on the road down, but Bob saw nobody in either direction. He hesitated. Should he chance staying on the road? It would be easier than cross-country travel. Since he wasn't hiking for pleasure, he decided that advantage outweighed risk.

On the road, his thoughts returned his reason for the trip, a visit to Clorinda Vinette's lodge. He'd search the house, room by room for some clue to Clorinda's murderer. The sheriff had probably been so intent upon convicting Bob that he carted away the body and the gun without further search.

A glance toward the sun told Bob it was past noon. He turned onto the lane that led to the lodge. Picking up his pace, he put thoughts of food out of his mind. Maybe he'd build a fire in the lodge's fireplace? What was the cook's name again? She and some of her friends could be squatting in the lodge. If there were smoke coming from a chimney, he'd have to reconsider his approach.

When he saw smoke rising from the chimneys, he stopped behind a stand of evergreens. He'd have people to question, but he wouldn't be able to search the house. The whole idea behind the trip was to search the lodge, and now he'd be thwarted from accomplishing anything. Frustrated, he pounded his fist into the palm of his hand.

He began to walk away, but stopped.

If the Indians occupied the lodge, he might be able to bluff and bluster them into answering questions and letting him search through the house. Bob wouldn't go away without getting inside the lodge, but first he'd scout around.

Staying hidden behind the trees and brush that surrounded the lodge, he trudged to various vantage points. He would have welcomed a pair of binoculars to get a closer peek, but finally, he decided that all the looking wouldn't get him inside, or help him to catch a murderer or a kidnapper.

Standing for a moment, he took a deep breath. What he found could mean the difference between a life of a fugitive and a life of freedom. He wouldn't back away, so he crossed the yard and took off his snowshoes. He climbed the steps to the door and knocked on it.

The echo of the knock had scarcely died away before the door opened a crack and the muzzle of a gun pointed out at him. "Come inside, Bob."

Bob thought he recognized the deep voice.

"But first, put up your hands."

Bob weighed his chances of escape, but, in the end, he raised his hands. The door swung wide open.

"You," Bob said, his eyes widening.

CHAPTER TWENTY-EIGHT
ONE RAINDROP FOUND

Packed down under the runners of the sleigh, the snow made a fast track, and the roan horse pulled the sleigh effortlessly. Marian was at the reins while the first light of morning ushered in a clear winter day. She urged the horse forward, and it responded by picking up speed.

"You'll land us in a drift, Marian," Alice Blue said, hanging on to the armrest. "There's no rush. It's not as though Bob is going anywhere."

"Bob was in that jail for over a month," Marian said. "Each time I saw him, he seemed more desperate. What went on in his mind? He kept everything to himself. I couldn't cheer him, no matter how I approached him.

"Now he's free. Maybe he will attempt something rash to make up for the time he was behind bars. I can't believe he'll ever be the cheerful Bob from before... I had difficulty stopping myself from dashing to him yesterday, but I waited for the heat of the search to die away. Do you understand why he and I must talk?"

Without waiting for an answer, she grabbed the whip and cracked it over the horse. The roan broke into a gallop.

"I'd do the same if I were you, but don't tip us. An accident could stop us altogether," Alice said.

Her cheeks rosy, Alice kept her hands warm inside a beaver muff. Snug inside a beaver coat and hat, she appeared to be warm while sedentary. Marian, on the other hand, had readied herself for an active day outdoors. She carried a tin of shortbreads, tea, matches, and a metal cup in her haversack, and she wore a heavy plaid mackinaw, wool trousers, leather pacs, and a tasseled knit tuque.

Occasionally, a sleigh or automobile appeared in front or behind them, but Marian hoped for complete privacy when she began her trek to Bob's camp. When they arrived at Chick's Oakwood Tavern, they turned onto the deserted forest road. The little used road led through the center of the forest. A single lane had been trampled. No doubt it took days after each fresh snow to make it passable.

"This road is a single rut," Alice said. "Do you expect me to turn the cutter around by myself?"

"I took you at your word when you told me that you could handle a horse and sleigh."

"I can, but I'll get stuck in a drift if I try to turn the sleigh around on this narrow road."

"There's ample room, but I'll lead the horse about before I set out." She breathed deeply, filling her lungs with the pure air. "What a wild and beautiful setting." She kept her attention fixed ahead and to the left. "But I'm not certain I can recognize the hill I have to skirt to reach Bob's hideout. I'm better able to say hideout now, but when this is over, I vow I'll never use that word again."

A thoughtful, troubled expression replaced the one of concerned frenzy that had been on Marian's face. "Where do we stop?" she asked aloud.

"This is a fine time to discover that a snow-covered countryside is much different from a green one. We may end up in Falls City, if it doesn't snow." Alice looked up at the blue sky, and shivered. "Here I sit, hands clenched hoping clouds and snow won't roll in, and you set out as though it's a balmy spring day."

"There! That's the hill. A path leads between those alders. Whoa, horse."

They stopped besides an opening between alders, no more than a dimple between mounds. Marian turned and grabbed a pair of bear paw snowshoes from behind her in the sleigh. She tucked them under her arm, jumped off the sleigh, grabbed the roan's halter, and led it in a half circle to face back east.

"How will you get back home?"

Marian didn't answer while she studied a compass. There was no doubt she had to travel in a southerly direction, but she didn't want

Northern Knights

to chance getting lost. "I'll have Bob guide me to Chick's Tavern. We'll arrange transportation from there."

Marian dropped the bear paws onto the road, wiggled her feet into the fastenings, and adjusted the buckles. She waved heartily and smiled as Alice disappeared around a bend in the road. Suddenly she felt totally alone in the great emptiness of snow. No use worrying. Haversack on her shoulder, she started her journey. To remain as fresh as possible, she maintained a long, slow swinging gait, which ate up the miles.

From the edge of the meadow, Marian looked over Bob's small settlement and found it inviting after the long hike. A fire would feel good on her stiff, cold fingers. She glided straight ahead toward the old log cabin.

Excited at the thought of surprising Bob, she hurriedly removed her snowshoes and leaned them against the log wall before going up the steps. The idea that Bob would be surprised made her smile, and the smile broadened while she knocked on the door.

From inside, she heard, "Now what? Are you back already, Bob?" The door swung open.

"Miss Marian!" Will Scathlock said, disbelief but no smile on his face. "Bob's not here. I don't expect you came to see me, but come on inside."

"Where is he?"

"He left as soon as it was light for who knows where. Said it was a hunting trip, but he talked about finding a raindrop in a river. Strange talk, but the outing 'll do him good. What do you think?"

Alarmed, Marian wondered if she completely understood. "Did he give you any hint where he was going or when he'd be back?"

"He told me he'd be back late tomorrow."

"Was he in a good mood?"

"He seemed to be. He thumped me on the back with his hand and got syrup on my union suit, in too much of a hurry to wash his hand, I suspect. Now my shirt sticks to my underwear. I might have to wash my union suit before spring."

Marian cringed, picturing his underwear in her mind's eye.

She had to find Bob, so she had decided to locate his tracks and follow them. If she told Will, he'd certainly try to dissuade her. "I believe I'll turn around and go back. But first, I'm hungry." She shed her coat and sweater while talking. "What do you have that won't take too long to prepare?"

"How about a can of beans and home baked bread?"

Twenty minutes later, she waved good-by to Will. She plodded in the direction from which she had come, but when she got beyond the ring of trees rimming the glade, she began to circle it attempting to cut Bob's trail. She was three hours behind him, but he had broken trail. A quarter mile of trudging brought her to a fresh trail.

A look at her compass told her the trail went northwest. Where was he going?

Bob's reason for such a trip worried her, too. Was he depressed enough to make fatal mistakes in the harsh environment? What motivated him enough to take him into the wilderness? Six hours later she had an answer to the first question.

Bob's snowshoe trail beelined across an open field. On the other side, Marian recognized Clorinda Vinette's lodge. With Clorinda gone permanently, a person would have thought the house would have been cold and vacant, but the opposite appeared to be true. Smoke billowed from the stone chimney. Clorinda's servants must have squatted in the lodge.

What could Bob hope to find there? Marian wavered. Would Bob want her following him?

Bob's trail circled the building, but eventually led to the front door. Black ominous clouds were blotting out the blue sky. Marian shivered. Something told her not to approach the front door. Lamplights flickered inside the house, and Marian decided to peek through a window when she reached the building.

Even with darkness descending, Marian would stand out as a black shadow against the white snow if she tried crossing the stark field. Toward the lake, she saw several clumps of birches. Using them for cover would take her on a roundabout route, but she thought she'd be hidden from view from the house until she got close enough for a dash across the yard.

Breathing hard from the dash, she caught her breath before leaning against the house and removing her bear paws. She edged up to the lighted window. Most of the window was frosted over, but Marian could see Bob. Hair tousled and cheeks ruddy, he sat on a wooden bench, facing a high-backed chair with a lamp table next to it. He seemed to be alone. Then, what looked like an elbow rested on the arm of the high-backed chair, and a puff of smoke wreathed the chair. A hand holding a pipe appeared from behind the high back of the chair.

She could see into the room, but she couldn't hear voices. Turning her face, she pressed her ear close to the pane behind the frost.

The voices were hollow. She barely recognized Bob's voice, but she did understand what was being said.

"I trust your meal was a pleasant one. We wanted to show you that we are civilized even under the present conditions."

Bob cleared his throat. "You did that, but I was the most surprised man on the planet when you opened that door and pointed your gun at me. Tell me, was money your only motive for the kidnapping?"

"Not that I have to tell you anything, but there's no need to be rude or secretive, anymore. I was desperate for the wealth that was slipping through my fingers, and you people were of no help with your well wishes. Nothing helped until I hit upon what I supposed was a foolproof scheme."

They stopped talking, but Marian heard a clink. Raising her eye to her peephole in the center of the pane, she saw an ember drop from the pipe and land in the ashtray. Bob's lips moved. Again she put her ear to the frozen glass.

"You were too tenacious always trying to find the kidnappers, but Nat Mutch informed me of your comings and goings. I arranged Joe's murder to put you in jail months ago, but you escaped. Then justice triumphed when Sheriff Blue captured you. Our friend Nat told me your gang intended to break you out of jail, and I planned your demise, figuring it was the only way to stop you. But your luck prevailed again. Now you're in my hands, and luck won't save you."

"Why did you kill Joe?"

"He was useful but greedy. I had already given him five hundred dollars, but he wanted more. Then you came along, a fugitive in the forest.

Northern Knights

You were perfect to take the blame. Nat and I arranged your meeting with Clorinda. If it hadn't been the day of your bank robbery, it would have happened elsewhere.

"Dear Clorinda. She was in love with me, you know? She thought we'd go away together when the ransom was paid. When sweet Marian and the sheriff came around investigating Joe's death, she became, how do you say? Unraveled. She'd wanted to go to the sheriff. Her change of heart brought about her end sooner than I had planned. Nat wasn't able to inform me you were at the bank again that night. No matter. You're still the one wanted for murder.

"Now that you're privy to my activities, I have a question to ask you before I… How did you happen to snoop about here today?"

"While I was in jail," Bob said, "I had time to think. It seemed so much action happened here that there should be a clue to the mystery around here, somewhere. I was sure right about that."

"Dead right, but I won't kill you here, unless you force me to. I don't want to clean up blood again.

"My wife tells me that the full ransom has been raised, and I'll be able to collect it after my next demand. I love winning. You'll be perfect as one of the kidnappers, but I don't want to keep you alive until then, I respect your tenacity. You'll keep admirably frozen outdoors until needed.

It's time now. Get up."

Marian put her eye to the peephole. Bob was on his feet. His captor stood. My God, Richard King. He'd staged his own kidnapping. What were they waiting for? Could Celeste King be somewhere close by? Richard had to be provisioned somehow. Where was his wife?

A voice from behind her answered her question. "Who are you? Get Up."

Marian's heart stopped. She and Bob were both prisoners. Turning her head, she buried her nose in her coat collar and glanced back to see where Celeste stood, a scant six feet away clad in a heavy sweater and trousers. Marian saw the futility of leaping at her.

"Raise your hands. Get up," Celeste repeated. "I can't miss at this distance."

This was no way to help Bob. She placed her hands on the snow covered sill in front of her and began to push herself upright. Snow! Marian filled both hands with snow. She'd surprise Celeste. If only she didn't shoot when her eyes were full of snow, Marian's plan might work.

Marian spun about.

"Why, it's sweet Marian."

Marian unleashed both crude snowballs at the same time. They both hit Celeste King directly in her face. Marian leaped at her, grabbed her gun hand, and wrenched the weapon away from the little carrot-topped woman. Marian flung the gun it into the snow. Celeste tried to wrestle herself free of Marian's grasp, clawing at her in vain.

Celeste gasped. "Damn you."

Grabbing her by her shoulders, Marian flung Celeste against the house. Celeste tried to run, but Marian grabbed her hand and whirled her through the window.

The crash startled both Richard King and Bob. Frozen in place, Richard turned from Bob. His mouth hung open, his gaze fastened on his wife.

Bob leaped at Richard, delivering a roundhouse right to Richard's ear. He toppled to the floor. The thirty-eight-caliber pistol skittered over the floor. Dazed, Richard crawled across the floor on his hands and knees to retrieve the pistol. Bob latched his right hand onto Richard's belt, yanked him back, and to his feet. They faced each other again.

Richard said, "You son of a bitch. Is there no end to your luck?" His eyes were glazed, and he swayed from side to side. He lurched toward Bob swinging his fists wildly. Bob stepped inside the feeble blows and smashed an uppercut to Richard's midriff. Richard doubled over, gasping.

Drawing his right hand back, Bob whistled a punch that crashed on the side of Richard's jaw, almost tearing his head from his shoulders.

Richard dropped to the floor, unconscious, and Bob stood over him.

Marian vaulted through the window and into Bob's waiting arms.

Bob looked at Marian. "How did you?"

"No talk," She said. "Kiss me,"

CHAPTER TWENTY-NINE
EVERYONE CAME FOR THE WEDDING

Peaceful days had settled on Gamwell County while Bob and Marian prepared for a June wedding.

June tenth in 1933 was a perfect Saturday. No clouds marred the blue sky that afternoon. Soft breezes wafted through the open casement windows and played about the steeple of the Church at the Corners.

Bob stepped to the window of the second floor room where he and Will waited for the ceremony to begin. Green meadows and woodland framed the Moose Ear River, which was back within its banks after an early spring flood. To the south, the trunk highway carried no traffic. To the north, the people of Langston listened to the community band in the square.

Rising from his chair, Will joined Bob at the window. "So you and Marian are heading north for your honeymoon?"

Bob smiled. "That's right. Marian and I have a room reserved at Bald Eagle Lodge on Madeline Island in the Apostles. I chartered a boat to take us there. Leo Long Mane lives on another island in the Apostles now, and works for a recluse. The old man's been feuding with everybody who settles on the island, which appropriately is known as Hermit Island. We may look Leo up while we're there. He says someone's teaching him to write."

Thinking of Leo turned his thoughts to the ordeal he and Marian had gone through. He tried to keep from thinking about it, but thoughts insinuated themselves too often.

" There's the music. Come on, Bob."

The two men hurried down the wooden steps to the front of the church, their new black shoes creaking as much as the stairs.

The day Bob had eagerly awaited finally arrived. He and Marian Alcott were to be married. With Bob at the altar for the double ceremony were his best man, Will, the other groom, Mike Rood, and his best man, Cal Little. While turning to watch Marian, Bob dug his hand into his trouser pocket and twisted the gold wedding band between his fingers. Will refused to hold the wedding band, saying he'd sure loose it or drop it or something.

The strains of the "Wedding March," a trifle tinny, played on an upright piano accompanied Marian and the other bride, Alice Blue, down the aisle.

Bob turned his attention to the crowd. Friends and neighbors packed the church. His mother wore a pale yellow dress. She had traveled in from Rapid City, South Dakota with her rancher husband. Bob was thankful she'd been able to attend the wedding.

Also there, dressed in green, was Grace Quennel. With the King brothers in prison, she had purchased the King Mercantile Bank, and ran the bank for the benefit of the community.

Arm and arm with her father, Marian beamed through her veil. A smile was painted on Jeffery Alcott's face. It had to be painted on because it wasn't possible that he could smile for more than a moment.

After standing together as they had, Marian knew she and Bob were going to be partners in their marriage. She smiled at Bob. She wouldn't miss her teaching post quite as much as she had thought because her school board position, though part time, would keep her active.

Of course, there was the honeymoon first. The Bald Eagle Lodge was famed for its food and accommodations. They would see the sights together. Together was most important.

At the altar, Jeffery Alcott released Marian's hand to Bob, and Roland Blue released his daughter's hand to Mike Rood. He shook Mike's hand before stepping aside. Roland Blue had opened a detective agency in Milwaukee and no longer lived in Gamwell County.

The music stopped, and the ceremony began. A new chapter in their lives was about to begin, strengthened by the trials they'd endured together since last September. Bob slipped the gold wedding band on Marian's finger. Before they knew it, the ceremony ended.

They kissed, then walked up the aisle together.

The End

ABOUT THE AUTHOR

A graduate of Morton College in 1960, Ed Pahnke has since completed a wide array of courses and seminars. He entered banking in 1961 and has been auditor at three banks over the years.

His first short story appeared in "Et Al" in 1971, and he subsequently had a number of short stories and articles published. In addition, he writes and edits a bimonthly newsletter.

Northern Knights, results from his fascination with and love for Wisconsin's North Woods, the 1930's, and the Robin Hood legends. A second Bob Brunet mystery, *Hermit Island*, is in progress.

Pahnke fully expects to keep writing fiction and nonfiction until ginkgo biloba is no longer effective, at which time he'll run for public office.